Raised by New York

22 Unexpected Journeys

Raised by New York

22 Unexpected Journeys

Herve Bebele

Copyright

Dedication

In memory of my daughter, Bebe, who inspired me to write and tell my life's stories.

To my wife, Arda, for supporting me through all my childish temper tantrums and staying with me until I discovered for myself the satisfaction of writing a good story. Thank you.

To Phyllis, Linda, Sonia, Hank, Susan, Julie, Bobbi, and others in my writing group who have come and gone. Thank you.

Table of Contents

Foreword

These stories are descriptive snapshots of my journey through life. I am now past the halfway point and it is joyful to look back and rediscover those *moments*, the stepping-stones, to the present. Sometimes, I stayed on a stone for years before I moved to another.

New York was my world. I grew up in Brooklyn when farms raising cows and horses dotted the southern parts of Brooklyn and Queens. The stories give a glimpse into my schooling, neighborhood, and the beehive of activity that was New York, then and now. It was in the big apple that I launched my business career, met Arda, and began to raise a family.

My existential journey through the years of dancing the Argentine Tango broadened my appreciation for the beauty in art, dance, and the unmanageable passion of the tango.

I learned and accepted the metaphysical demands my body asked of me while training to be a winning road bicyclist.

Now that I have time to reflect, the desire to tell my stories to others, and most notably to my grandchildren, blossomed into a memoir of my life—real and imagined.

"Women and Weed" tells the story of a man in mid-life becoming involved with the cannabis craze and the women who sold it. Their goal was to improve their lives in the city's most populous boroughs: The Bronx and Brooklyn. This story is sexually explicit and contains language of the city. Names and specific locations may have been changed to protect the identity of individuals in the stories.

The Tom Turkey

It is difficult to picture a more blissful scene: a dozen or so hens along with two turkeys free grazing on two acres of sun-soaked grass, two five-gallon pails of water to quench their thirst and two feeding trays full of food. I wanted my egg-laying hens to feel complete contentment in their surroundings. My family and friends loved the fresh eggs I gathered every morning. They were very pretty, they varied in color from light blue to golden brown with speckled eggs from the turkey adding to the variety.

My daily routine varied only slightly. A few more eggs, a little less chicken poop, more sun, less rain. Even the walk from the house to the coop was just the right distance.

The birds were free-ranging throughout the property, so there was enough room for all, and it also kept the chicken fights to a minimum. My attention was always on the safety of the birds. This meant that the fence and the hen house be adequately secured against raccoons, wolves, and the ever present hawkers from above.

I was, as they say, tending my chickens, and since I did not have a working rooster, I appreciated the Tom Turkey watching over the "hen house." His relationship with his ladybird was a typical one. He took care of her safety and she put up with all of his macho crap. The hens were content with the "pecking order" in the hen house. He was their alpha male. Over time, maybe a year or so, my relationship and impression of the Tom turkey changed from a benevolent caretaker of twelve hens and his lady to a life threatening menace to the hens and me. Somewhere in his DNA, he perceived me as a threat to his authority. No matter what I did or did not do, I was his competitor, a threat to rule the roost.

It was mid-summer when I began to notice the Tom following me whenever I approached the run leading into the hen house. I thought he was fulfilling his duties as the guardian of the flock. On a few occasions, as I was cleaning up the poop or changing the water, I felt him leaping at me from behind, and in turning around, it was exactly that. He was attacking me. I began to carry a stick, and when I felt him getting too close, I would turn and sure enough he was in flight—and if I had not turned, he would have landed on my back. I would swat at him and he would back off a bit, but he still remained close enough to make another jump at me. Once I realized that I was in a hostile and combative relationship, I paid much closer attention to the Tom.

I could not believe that he was attacking me, but he was. I thought I had become delusional. I then noticed that he was actually tracking my movements well before I entered the run.

I started to talk to him thinking this might help, but his aggression toward me never changed. In talking to him I began to tell him that I was going to eat him on Thanksgiving Day. I described the Thanksgiving dinner to him and brought in a calendar of the year and pinned it onto the wall. I opened the calendar to the month of November and highlighted the 25th. I highlighted the day in blood red India ink and circled it as well. The Tom watched me pin and circle the date. When I pointed out the date to him, he went nuts. He started jumping all around the hen house and flew back and forth to the end of the run all the while cackling in his loudest cackle. I ran around him, shouting: "Thanksgiving is just a couple of months away, and you're going to be dinner." He would go nuts when I talked to him like that. I left the hen house having fed the birds and given them enough water for the evening. I closed the coop and the run and went back to the house, finished for the day and feeling good about tomorrow.

3

The next day I let the birds out about 7 a.m. and went to collect the eggs. I noticed the calendar had been torn off the wall and the month of November was ripped into a thousand pieces. As I stared, stunned at what he had done, I noticed the Tom watching me from the run. He did not move and never took his eyes off me. I did not know whether to laugh or cuss at the Tom.

I bought another calendar and wrapped the month of November in thin plexiglass. I circled the 25th again and mounted the plexi-piece into the wall. During the month of October, the Tom and I just shadowed each other. I always carried a stick, and when I sensed he was getting ready to attack, I turned and swung my stick. Many times I caught him in midair coming at my back. I got very close to hitting him but never did, although I did scare him. Then came the month of November. I bought a permanent ink red marking pen and made a big x on the first of November. The Tom was watching me, and when he saw me cross out the first of November and recognized its relationship to the 25th which did not yet have a cross but a circle, he started to fly into the wall again and again cackling all the time.

All the birds in the run were scared. Really scared; their feathers were matted, and they were all huddled in a corner near the exit door of the run. The Tom finally settled down and just stared at me. His eyes were now blood red. I went about my end-of-the-day business and locked the birds up for the night. The next morning, I let the birds out. They were very happy to leave the hen house and get into the run. I saw the Tom watching me from the run; I saw him watching me cross out November 2nd with my red marker. I walked out of the shed and into the run. The Tom flew directly at the calendar and tried to scratch out the cross I had just made. He was screaming, and for the first time, I saw him kicking up the hay and the shit on the floor onto the calendar. His eyes were changing colors as they focused on me. His gullet was pulsing like a heart. I thought it was growing.

Was I dreaming? Was I in a battle with a Tom turkey who understands the meaning of my Thanksgiving calendar and how the 25th of November could possibly have an impact on him?

The morning scenario repeated itself every day for the next twenty-one days. He would be kicking and cackling furiously. On the morning of November 23rd, I came into the house and saw the female turkey lying on the floor under the plexi-calendar with her gullet ripped out. The Tom was standing over her. I looked up at the calendar and saw he had pecked a dozen or so holes into the plexi-calendar around the number 25. The holes were red; it was the blood of his woman. I understood what the Tom had done: he had sacrificed his lady bird in his place and hoped that it would be enough for me.

I looked directly at the Tom. He had big tears running down his eyes. I know this is impossible, but that is what I saw. Strange thoughts started to run through my mind. It was then and there that I knew what had to be done. Later that night, I went back to the hen house, a little after 10 p.m. The moon was still high in the sky. I had taken a winter car blanket with me. I carefully opened the door to the hen house and knowing where the Tom's position on the roost was, I threw the blanket over him. I made sure I had his legs wrapped securely. I could hear his breathing through the blanket. He was not fighting; that meant he was still sleepy.

I had parked the car on the grass near the chicken shed with the engine running. The trunk was open and there was a large-sized crate in it. It was easy to put the Tom into the crate and close the trunk. I drove about twenty minutes to a secluded wooded area that is part of the water shed system in upstate New York. I took the Tom from the trunk and slowly lifted the blanket off him. It was in the eye of moonlight that I saw the Tom look directly into my eyes, and the color of his eyes changed from fiery red to a soft grey. He turned away from me and walked off. Freedom.

The Trash Collector

Most of the eight families living along Flat Bottom Road have been there long enough to see the young sprouts of Douglas fir reach forty to fifty feet high. This rural realm of tranquility and beauty is but sixty miles from New York City, located straight up the Hudson River, opposite the fabled Bear Mountains. You can get to Flat Bottom by train from New York City in a little less than an hour. One would think that in this piece of heaven on earth that *living* would be harmonious, pacific, and even boring. Ha.

Nobody quite remembers when recycling first began, but we remember that time as the beginning of our collective morning anxiety attacks.

Recycling household waste required three different colored trash pails: one for garbage, the second for paper, and the third for metal, plastic and glass. It also required three different pickup days. Tuesday was garbage pickup day, Wednesday paper, and Thursday was reserved for inorganic waste. The town sanitation department prepared its pickup schedule based on the time the sun rises. In the winter your pickup time might fall from 8 a.m. on. As the sun rose earlier and earlier, your pickup time could shift to as early as 7 a.m. In the summer the range would be 7:30 a.m. to 8:30 a.m. If this is confusing to you, just think how confusing it was to me and the lovely lady lying beside me. She remained in a perpetual, heightened state of anxiety, worrying about the different pickup days.

The garbage truck was a big truck—too big for Flat Bottom Road. It had a loud diesel engine and squeaky brakes. You could hear it coming a good half mile away and could tell what part of the road it was on when it started to back up to get around the curves in the road and into the intricate driveway patterns. With its automatic backup warning whistle, you could tell how far it was from your house. All of this information is very important if you intended to get your garbage picked up.

During the cold winter months, when there is usually some ice or snow on the ground, the garbage truck would come barreling down the road between 7:45 and 8 a.m. In these months it gets light at about 7:30 a.m. This knowledge of morning light is important. You cannot, under any circumstances, put the garbage out the night before, or even in the early morning hours, if it's still before sun up.

Why is that important, you ask? Because the raccoons are out until first light and they will rip your pail apart and spread your garbage all over the road. I've tried everything—bungee cords, metal pipes to the handles, locks on top, even hazardous materials—to take out the 'coons. However, nothing works.

The winter weather didn't help either. Over time, the blacktop buckled, cracked, and eventually disappeared. The road, now looked like it had a century ago. Rocks, ruts, and dirt. The extreme temperature conditions had eroded the colors on the three trash barrels. All were now a dirty grey.

Over the years, you learned to get up in the cold early mornings as soon as you heard the truck barreling down the road. You knew you had to get the garbage down. If they don't see the garbage pail at the foot of your driveway, they keep on moving. In fact, I thought they liked that. Maybe they were trying to mess with your head—you know, like no pickups on Flat Bottom Road today.

This behavior morphed into an unspoken agreement. If they could get to the road before the usual time, and while you were still in bed— they would see a man in their rearview mirror, running down the drive, dragging a pail full of a week's garbage, in his bare feet, waving and trying to whistle over the roar of the diesel as it flew by. I swear that you say to yourself, "They are coming earlier this winter!" Now you just have to take the pail back up the drive and store it until next Tuesday. You can imagine what the garbage will smell like by the second week. Tuesday morning becomes an important moment in your "lives." I say "lives" because the lady of the house occasionally has nightmares and inquires in the middle of the night if you've taken out the garbage. Or she hears the truck, or she thinks she hears the truck. Any one of these scenarios presents a nightmare in progress.

As the years passed, you could see that all the families had gotten into the routine of getting up right after sunrise and, in their own way, would bring the trash down to the side of the road. You could almost set your clock to the big trash truck barreling down the road.

But, every now and then, they would come early, as much as an hour early. It was as if they'd forgotten to set their clocks; or, maybe they were just being nasty that morning. Nevertheless, still asleep, you heard them coming. When this happened you could almost hear the screams in all the family bedrooms along Flat Bottom Road: "Get the garbage! Get the garbage! They're coming!"

This is when the image of the story presents itself in full splendor: Eight men in their briefs, usually in bare feet, running like hell, dragging one, sometimes two pails behind them, each hoping the other will get to the road and slow down the trash truck with its burly driver and two helpers. If we can make it to the road, we win this week's trash battle. If they succeed in getting past us before we get to the road, you will clearly see a smile on their faces. That is, until the following week.

A Lesson Learned

My older brother Jerome and I were among the few paying students in a private parochial school supported by the largest Jewish organization in New York City. This institution was known for taking in orphans and new arrivals from Eastern Europe.

The Yeshiva, as it was called, had one hundred fifty students spread over grades one through six. The building was impressive—a stone structure rising more than three stories high in this quiet Brooklyn residential neighborhood. It once had classrooms on all three floors; however, all of the first floor had been reconfigured into three large rooms, the largest of which became the sanctuary and prayer area for both the school and the neighborhood. The other two rooms became the principals' offices of the Hebrew and English departments. Hebrew classes were on the second floor and English classes on the third.

I remember it being fun running down the stairs from the third floor to the schoolyard and up again to the third floor. The stairway was very wide, almost twice the width of a traditional one. It must have had a grand purpose at one time. Two, maybe three, students could run alongside each other as they bolted from floor to floor.

The school day was divided into morning and afternoon sessions. The morning session was devoted to Bible studies, Hebrew history, and the study of the Talmud (Jewish law). We studied the history of every holiday found in the Bible. There were many. The classes were excruciatingly boring and repetitive.

If any day of the year was important, it was the first day of school—the day you selected your seat. The choice was critical. The seat and desk you picked were yours for the entire school year. At the beginning of each and every year, I chose a window seat.

My interest lay in looking out the window and watching the girls play in their schoolyard across the street. They looked so happy, always smiling and laughing. Counting cars and guessing even or odd license plate numbers filled in my time when the girls were in their classes. Fire trucks and police cars with their sirens blasting added to my reverie.

The Rabbi was not fooled. He knew. Now and then when he saw I was in "la land," he would quietly walk up behind me and punch me in the shoulder, or shake my shoulders, or bang the desk with his ruler. Sometimes, he would put his face next to mine and say, "So, Herschel," (that was my Hebrew name), "vat vas so important that you are looking so hard out the vindow? You spend all your time looking out the vindow. Maybe I should change your seat. No?" I never looked up. I had heard those words before. "No, Rabbi, I thought I saw a man steal a woman's pocketbook, that's all."

I was not studious, but I was a bright kid, and I learned the important stuff by listening. It helped that I had a good memory and was naturally street smart. My brother and I shouldn't have been in a religious school as we were troublemakers and certainly not religious. My parents were not Orthodox; they just wanted to send their children to a good school. Living in Brownsville meant the choices were very limited. My brother wasn't interested in girls. He was, however, interested in fighting. Needless to say, the last name "Hunt" was not held in high regard by the faculty at the Yeshiva. On the contrary, Jerome's interest in fighting was so pronounced that shortly after he finished the third grade, he was asked to leave the school.

My brother's expulsion put a cloud over my remaining years at school. Now, I would be the one they would watch with suspicion. Still, life at school had been good until one fateful day in my fourth grade Hebrew class. I remember it as if it happened this morning. I sat down at my desk and slid my lunch and books onto the shelf under my desk. There, much to my surprise, I found a wad of bubble gum stuck to the upper inside of the shelf. As fortune would have it, the Rabbi was walking down the aisle just then. He noticed me reaching under my desk. He saw the gum. He may have thought I was putting the gum under the desk for safekeeping, or he may have thought I was using the cubby to discard the gum. Either way, he went nuts and smacked me across the face. He demanded that I apologize for chewing in class and for dirtying up the desk with my "sticky glob of goo."

This Rabbi did not look like the ones de-scribed in the Old Testament. Rabbi Hochmann was a short, thin man with a full beard of gray, straggly hair. His skullcap sat high on his head which was covered with the same stringy hair. He needed a haircut a long time ago. He fidgeted and paced, especially when he talked. His tongue would get in the way, and he would invariably spray his spittle all over you.

I tried to explain that it was not *my* gum. I knew that it must be a kid in the previous class who had put it there, but since I was in a different classroom for that period, I had no idea who that kid was. But the Rabbi had a suspect, and that was all he needed.

The smack across the face hurt and I was close to tears; it reinforced my opinion that I did not belong there.

The following morning, just as I was taking my seat, the Rabbi came down the aisle, put his hand underneath my desk, and again pulled out a wad of bubble gum. Furious, with a crazed expression on his face, he again, with an open hand, smacked me across the face. Hard. I began to cry.

He spent the next few minutes telling the class what a terrible thing I had done.

"It is against Jewish law—the Talmud. It is a sin, it is against school policy, and it is against this Rabbi's principles." He spoke so fast that the students couldn't understand him.

Thankfully, the bell rang; it was time for recess. Once on the field, I quickly forgot about his smack down—until the next morning.

As I entered the class, the Rabbi was already walking toward my seat, defeating my plan of checking underneath the desk before he had a chance to. I watched as he pulled out another wad of gum and again, with that crazed expression, he smacked me across the face. Hard. Crying, unable to control myself, I got up, and put my fist close to the Rabbi's face.

"You hit me again, and I'll punch you in the nose," I whispered, trying to catch my breath. The class understood you don't talk to a Rabbi like that. Ever. The Rabbi was frightened. He knew he had gone too far. Now he wanted to make nice. It seemed forever before he spoke.

"Come. Sit in the front row."

Only good students sat in the front row.

"You can read today's Bible portion." Again, only the good students got to read.

At the end of the morning session, the Rabbi approached me and told me that sitting in the front row made a difference in his opinion of me and that we, the Rabbi and I, should drop the gum issue and start over. He specifically made mention that he would not tell the principal or my parents and thought that I should not tell them either. To me, it sounded like a solution to a recurring nightmare. Moreover, I could concentrate on soccer during the morning recess.

The following morning, it was all smiles between the Rabbi and me. I was still sitting in the first row and again was called upon to read the portion of the Bible that the Rabbi was a specialist in. Time passed quickly, and all seemed to be well in the "Holy Land."

I loved jumping down the stairs to get to the schoolyard and get into the soccer game. I flew down the last ten steps, which were outside the building and led directly to the schoolyard. There on the third step, waiting for me, was my mother.

Now my mom was much tougher than the Rabbi. Look who she had to put up with—two delinquents. She grabbed me by the collar and said, "If I ever hear that you threatened a teacher again, what he gave you will be a love tap, a kiss on the cheek to what your father and I will do to you. Is that clear?" This was the first time my mother had been asked to come to school on my behalf. She released her choke hold on me and continued up the stairs into the building. I suspected she was going to see the Rabbi and tell him that she had talked to her son and that an incident like this would not *ever* happen again.

The Rabbi had lied to me and to my mother! He lied! The Rabbi represents God, and he lied! He just wanted to get to my mom before I did. I waited for my mom to come out, but she didn't come out through the schoolyard door. She must've used the main entrance to exit the school. At home, I tried my best to tell her my side of the story but to no avail. All she kept on repeating was, "You threatened a teacher; this is your first and last warning. You're just like your brother, a troublemaker, and I am not going to have two of them in my house."

I learned more than I thought I did from this experience. After the fourth grade, I understood that God was not on my side. That telling the truth paid few, if any, dividends and that *truth* and its sibling *trust* were no match for a corrupt authority and the administration of physical intimidation. Was this what I was supposed to learn?

A Prayer Answered

After learning, that God and I did not see eye to eye on questions of faith, my parents decided to give both of us another chance. Finishing elementary school education at the Yeshiva, they decided to send me to the "Mesivta," which had a similar educational structure of Hebrew and Bible studies in the morning and the required public school classes in the afternoon.

Deep down, my parents did not trust the educational values found in the public schools of Brooklyn. Brooklyn had a poor record of accomplishment in its educational system. It mirrored the expectations of how people felt about the safety of its streets. You learned to take care of yourself and to recognize "street situations" or else you paid the consequences. My parents felt the same concern regarding its education. Bullies were born, bred, and raised in Brooklyn.

My brother, Jerome, joined the local gang and gained a reputation as a tough street fighter. They called him "J", as he became known as the

Jew who could and would fight. His street creds threw a blanket of protection over me and our younger sister.

Choosing the Mesivta was a fortuitous choice for my parents as we had just moved into a two-family house. We still needed more room as my mom gave birth to our youngest brother. The school, however, was close by and I could walk there easily.

The school occupied the historical Stone Street building, an old textile plant on Stone Street. The first four floors were occupied by study halls, prayer halls, dining halls, and bathrooms. The top two floors were leftover from the days when the laborers at the factory did not go home and used the floors as sleeping dens. It insured the factory would have workers the next day. Now, they were dormitories for the students who were afraid to go out into the "blackboard jungle" neighborhood after school, and who were zealous enough not to want to drive on the holy days. It helped enrollment for the Mesivta to advertise safe live-in quarters available for out-of-state students.

I had just turned thirteen and was preparing to take the eighth grade exams in both Hebrew and English studies.

The Mesivta combined the middle and high school grades into a six-year program. The high school had the larger student population. It seemed, as you progressed into the upper class-man status, the more times a day you were required to pray. Four times a day was normal. If it were a holiday, they prayed non-stop. To me, they were always going to the prayer hall or the study hall.

Both halls were fertile areas to sell my *smut-filled character* comic books. Superman was dressed only in a red cape and showed Lois Lane what really made him super. I found it best to sell during school prayers.

"Shlomo, Shlomo! Wake up! I can't believe you're sleeping standing up! Open up your siddur, I have the new Dick Tracy and Wonder Woman comics for you."

Shlomo looked right and left to make sure he was not being watched. Surreptitiously he lowered his Siddur to accept the new issues.

"I pay you later, in the dining room." He mumbled.

"Ok, today. Don't be late."

I knew what *they* all thought of me. I was selling "dreck," smut, garbage, lustful images that were not in *their* bible. In their eyes, I was the devil. All the other students were dedicated to God and studies. Me, I was passing through, selling sex books to God's warriors.

These comic books were another form of *modern* day pornography. I found it to be a perfect after-school job. Studying and learning all about God was of no interest to me. As often happens, having almost finished *serving my time* without being caught, I was told to report to the principal's office before going to my next-to-last class.

The principal, Rabbi Fried, did not look up; he pointed to the chair in front of his desk and said, "Sit!"

Which I did.

Rabbi Fried was a big man, tall, slightly overweight, a full head of hair and a thick handlebar mustache. I had just turned thirteen and looked like ten.

He put the most recent comic books I had sold on his desk, in front of me, and said, "Where did you get these?"

"From a guy that sells apples off his pushcart. He comes once a month to Belmont Avenue and keeps the books under a blanket."

"What's his name? I want to know his name!"

"I don't know his name; sometimes he doesn't even come around."

"Herschell, I know your uncle Sammy; we went to school together and then into the army. We were good friends until he moved away to attend graduate school. Because of our friendship, you have two options First, tell me who you bought the comics from and I will take care of the matter myself and report him to the police. The second option, in respect for your uncle, is that you do not come back to my school in the fall. I will be clearer that you never come back to my school again. The school year is almost over and you will have all summer to find another high school to accept you. The choice is yours."

For me, the decision had already been made. "I will be going to a public high school in the fall."

"Good, you don't belong here." Never looking up, he began to shuffle papers on his desk. I guess that was his goodbye.

The school year ended, and I was off to a new house, new school, new friends, and new business adventures.

I realized, finally, that God was listening to me after all.

I Made My Mom Proud

Being the second son in my family made me automatically the first loser. All presents and gifts (expensive) went to my older brother. He didn't ask that it be that way, it just was.

Unknowingly, I harbored a resentment that most second and third children experience. I do remember being extremely competitive with my older brother which is one way I showed my unhappiness with second class citizenship.

Mom was a business woman and a mover in our local community. She had lots of friends. When we went food shopping for holidays or just to stock up on groceries, we would always run into them. After the most basic of greetings the conversation was always the same: "Esther, how are you? I haven't seen you for a long time. How is your family? What are the boys doing now? Are they still in school? Any lawyers or doctors in the family?" They completely ignored me as if I didn't exist.

Mom would answer: "The oldest is studying to be a scientist and the middle one we are not yet sure of" (that was me). This is how the conversation went no matter whom she was talking to. It was always the same. I heard it through my college years while I too studied science and graduated as a chemist.

I didn't last long as a chemist; I was more of a salesman, a social type, interested in people and not so much in science. So it was no surprise to my mother when I told her I had been fired from my first job at the chemical company and was going into the glue business with my brother (which didn't work out). Mom hardly mentioned me in her coffee klatch get together with her friends. When asked about me her response was always: "He's finding himself; it's taking longer than expected, but he's a good boy. He just needs more time."

Her eyes always looked at the floor or her coffee cup when she spoke of me; never into the eyes of the person who inquired about me. I know; I was there. It was not uncommon to become invisible to my parents' generation.

Life does move on, and I moved on within it. I met my wife, Arda, who is Dutch, a few years after finishing school. I started my own business of binding blank notebooks in very fancy fabrics for very fancy stationery stores. This put me into the gift and accessories industry rather than the chemical industry. Business was okay, just not enough money for a newly married man. As it happened, a salesman of mine in Boston (who sold my blank books) told me that most of his customers were looking for "love beads." This was the early 70s; everybody knew about flower power, love beads, and free love. After the usual chitchat, he mentioned there was a dearth of beads and an enormous demand for them. The person who could locate the source and supply them would make a lot of money.

We lived and worked in our one-bedroom apartment on 10th Avenue and 21st Street, not a good neighborhood. From there it was easy to walk to the millinery district in the 30s and inquire about beads in stores that sold needles, thread, buttons, and most importantly, decorative buttons. The decorative buttons looked like beads, and there were glass beads that were sold as buttons. I knew I was in the right market.

It was the end of October, and winter was on its way. Soon it wouldn't be easy to walk these streets. I covered a block of shops a day. Most stores did not carry "love" beads as an accessory, but they knew of the beads. On the third block, at the end of the third day, I had my first lead. The man spoke with a heavy European accent. He was difficult to understand, but not impossible. He said, "You go to Long Island City, look for the only varehouse building that has more than ten floors. You can't miss it. Go to the company called Needle Craft. Ask for a woman called Rosanna Rosanna."

That's what I heard. I thought I was playing a game "find the missing city." In the 70s I didn't think there was a building in Long Island City that had ten floors. LIC, then, was a vacant area whose only claim to fame was that it connected Queens to Manhattan via the 59th Street Bridge.

All the while, I had called other salesmen around the country and inquired if they too had a demand for "love" beads. All responded with a "will take as many as you can deliver."

With a couple of hundred dollars in my pocket, and the aspirations of good fortune, I drove my wife's VW to Long Island City. To me, it was like visiting one of those bombed out East German cities I had seen on television. No trees, no parks, very few people walking the streets. Desolation!

I went and did find the ten storied 'varehouse,' and yes, it was the only warehouse with ten stories. There were plenty of parking spaces for my VW beetle. The sign, although decrepit and illegible, (mostly) did lead me to the building's freight elevator.

I remembered the information: tenth floor. When I pulled the elevator door open directly in front of me, a blonde woman was sitting behind an old style conference table. It certainly wasn't a reception desk.

"What do you want?" She asked. She didn't bother with "hello" or "can I help you?"

I answered, "I'm looking for Rosanna Rosanna."

"Why?"

"I was told she has beads, love beads, and I want to buy some. I have cash."

"Everybody has cash, but I'm out of beads, don't have any right now."

"Are you Rosanna?" I asked. She didn't answer.

Rosanna didn't smile; not smiling went along with her bleached blond hair and thick reading glasses. But she didn't throw me out either. "How do you know I have beads?"

"I saw two guys loading their van in the parking lot. They were from Canada. I figure if they came all the way from Canada and left with beads, you have beads."

"Okay, Okay," she said in a loud, piercing voice. "Go upstairs to the 11th floor; take no more than 20 kilos. Choose your own colors and bring the bags back to me. I'll total you out. And don't come back!"

They had a secret eleventh floor!

Success! I had this big shit-eating grin on my face which she saw and then actually smiled.

"Rosanna," I said, "We're gonna be good friends before this is all over."

She didn't answer. I came down about a half hour later pushing a small cart filled with one kilo bags of glass beads. They were all colors:

31

pink, violet, royal blue, bright green, white, purple, black, and ruby red. That was a good beginning. She asked for three dollars a kilo. I gave her that, and a five-dollar tip. The tip made her smile. When she smiled, she radiated a different persona entirely. I decided to ask her the question of how she came to have a first and last name that was the same—"Rosanna Rosanna."

She smiled, "Many people would like to ask that question, you are one of the few that did. I married a man from Puerto Rico by the name of Fernando Rosannah. My luck! I get stopped at airports, banks and other places where you have to present identification. There are many crazy stories out there about my name; all are untrue, except my good fortune of marrying Fernando. So, Rosanna Rosannah, except for the *h*, it spells the same and sounds the same."

Part one of the three-part puzzle solved. Now I had to find a company that sold plastic vials or test tubes. Finally, I needed a cork to fit the test tube and the puzzle would be complete. I accomplished parts two and three with the assistance of the yellow pages. During the 70s every business advertised in the yellow pages. It was, as they said, "Let your fingers do the walkin'."

My apartment was too small to hold the bead supplies I recently purchased. This left little room to fill the expected orders. I needed more space. Thankfully, New York had a ton of warehouse spaces in Chelsea. I found a commercial building that specialized in 15' x 15' rooms with loading dock and wide walkways to maneuver freight from the elevator to your room. This would be very helpful later on.

As I said it was close to winter and when I put everything together, it was already early December. Arda and I had planned to go to Holland for the Christmas holidays. It would be my first trip to the Netherlands and the first opportunity to meet her family since we married six months ago.

All the shipping supplies—tape, cartons, shipping labels, scale, beads, tubes, and corks were in my warehouse room, #302. I took care of setting up UPS and Con Ed, opened a bank account, telephone account, and then finally signed the landlord's lease. I was ready.

The orders started to come in, most by first class mail from the salesman in the Boston area. It didn't take long to sell all the beads I bought from Rosanna. By the end of the first week, I made my second trip to Long Island City. No delays this time. I picked up 30 kilos of beads, paid cash, and was on my way back to the city. Easy enough. My bead business was C.O.D. (checks accepted). I went to the bank every day even if it was to deposit just one check. A gross of beads sold for $144.00, weighed four pounds with the carton, and I shipped the same day I received the order. I was making gross boxes of beads all day long (inventory). It was busy. Money was coming in: However, the closer we came to Christmas, the slower the incoming orders became. This was to be expected. Stores needed to sell the beads they bought.

All elements required to run my new business were successfully in place. It was time to find somebody to take care of the Christmas period in the warehouse while I went to Holland to meet Arda's family.

Mom just sold her apartment building (six apartments), and I knew she wouldn't mind helping her second child, the problem child, for a couple of weeks while I traveled to Europe. The day before leaving, I met her in room #302 to review the basics of opening the mail, shipping a couple of bead orders (the beads were already packed for shipping) and depositing the checks. She understood everything that needed to be done.

We agreed she did not have to come in every day, nor did she have to be there at 9 a.m. Noon would be fine. The mail came around 11 a.m. and was slipped under the door if the office was not yet open. I gave her the keys to the office and the telephone number to Arda's parent's home.

She asked, "Should I know anything else?"

34

I replied, "We'll be home before you know it."
I kissed her goodbye and told her I would send a
post card from Holland.

Holland was wonderful. The Dutch are
friendly, warm, outgoing people. I didn't speak
Dutch, and they didn't speak English all that
well, so I did a lot of sightseeing while 'the
family' did a lot of eating, talking, and drinking.
Everybody had a good time. I had money in the
bank, in my pocket, and no worries about business in New York. Arda and I would welcome
the New Year in Holland.

Sitting around the Jenikins living room,
listening to Arda's family and friends talk about
their childhood experiences (in Dutch), I felt
like a fly on the wall, quietly absorbing my first
European experiences. My equanimity was dis-
turbed by the loud ring of the telephone. Poppa
Jenikins answered the phone and called Arda
to take the call. Surprisingly, she called me to
the phone and whispered, "It's your Mother."

I whispered back, "My mother?" As she
passed the phone to me.

"Hi mom, you know it's 11 p.m. over here. Is
everything ok? What's going on?"

"My son, you're crazy and don't know it. I
have been in your office for more than a week. I
have been without beads for the last three days.
I shipped and sold all the beads you had. I
thought you said, 'Not to worry mom; business

would be quiet until after the New Year!' In the meantime, the phones are ringing off the hook; people are sending money by check, cash, and Western Union. They want beads.

"The UPS driver is mad because he cannot make your pick up the last one of the day anymore; you have too many packages. The landlord is angry because we put the boxes outside the room, so we can work inside, and he wants to charge you more rent for that. The garbage man is angry because you use his pails for your boxes and bead bags, and it leaves no room for the other tenants' garbage. Con Edison wants a larger deposit and so does AT&T. They say we are using too much electricity. My friends are angry because they are helping me pack beads when they should be home watching their grandchildren. And the customers are angry because we have no beads. So, give me your supplier's information; tell me how to get to them, and who to talk with. I will lay out the money; buy beads, tubes, corks, boxes, tape and labels.

"You're not normal, how could you leave a business like this and go off to Europe. The people are throwing money at you, a lot of money. I don't know why, but you struck gold selling beads. In fact, I think it's better than selling gold. I'm very impressed."

I gave her all the information and told her to put her faith in Rosanna for the selection of colors. However difficult it was, to do so over a long distance telephone line, I apologized for leaving her so unprepared, and thanked her for filling in while we vacationed in Europe. She hung up the phone before I could properly say goodbye.

Yes, I remember the time I was in the living room with my mom and her friends and heard her try and explain my business to them. I can still picture the women listening intently as she explained in her kind of look-and-listen-to-me voice. "It's unbelievable, all the money my son was making from little glass beads. He's a good businessman and very successful." Mom had a big smile on her face and made all of these hand gestures to show how much better things were now since I left the chemical business. "I am happy now," she said.

I'm sure I was blushing to hear her talk about me that way. The bead business brought stature and respect to me and my newly forming family. My Mom's freshly found pride and admiration for me lasted until she passed, thirty years later. In her eyes, and mine, I was now equal in her love and stature to my oldest brother. The sibling hierarchy had changed. Miracle of miracles!

I would like to think there were other times during those intervening years, before she passed, that I made her proud of me. But the bead adventure was the first and most important. It was the first step in a long journey.

The hysteria and demand for all styles, sizes, and shapes of beads kept me busy throughout the 70s. The fad quietly passed into history along with free love and cheap gas. With the money I made selling beads, we bought our house in the suburbs and moved out of Hell's Kitchen.

Mom loved to visit!

Morning Coffee

In the winter of '07, I began to awaken at sunrise, in the cold stillness of the early morning. I don't know why; maybe it was an effect from my latest trip to China. The time difference will play havoc with anybody's circadian cycle. But, whatever the reason, the die was cast. I was up at sunrise every day thereafter.

There was no sense in just tossing and turning. Worse, it would be unimaginable, turning on the light to read. That being said, I knew that when I got up, the dear woman next to me would also get up. That's just how we lived on Flat Bottom Road.

Given that we both liked a cup of espresso coffee in the morning, I decided to go downstairs (in my bare feet to stay silent) and fix a cup of espresso for the both of us. To make a fine pot of espresso, you need fresh cold country well water, good coffee beans, and a coffeepot—a mocha pot to be specific. Altogether, it takes about five minutes for the coffee to come to a boil. I cleaned the pot every day so there was no residue from the morning before.

Adrianne takes her coffee black with a sugar substitute. I take mine black. In order not to confuse which cup has the sugar I always take a horizontally striped mug for Adrianne and a vertically striped mug for me. That way I don't have to remember which is hers and which is mine. This is an organizational must.

With the coffee prepared, I tear a sheet of toweling off the roll for her and for me. By this time, it was light enough, and I made my way upstairs to our bedroom. Adrianne smelled the aroma as I walked up the thirteen steps balancing a cup of coffee in each hand. When I entered the bedroom there she was, sitting straight up in bed, resting her back against an oversized pillow. A big smile spread across her face. Looking in her eyes, you could see she was still dreaming.

"Good Morning," I said, as I presented her with the goods in my left hand. She took the toweling and spread it across her lap like a makeshift tabletop. Then she securely grasped the cup of coffee and placed it on the ledge of the bed. I went to my side of the bed where I lay on my side looking out the window at the bare trees and tasted the coffee—smooth, velvety, and strong. When the last sip was gone, I would always say: "Boy I could use a little more," but it was enough.

When I turned to Adrianne, her smile said it all. She could not stop telling me what a treat it was being served a fresh cup of coffee in bed at sunrise, surrounded by the winter outside.

Repeatedly, she whispered seductively, "Honey this is the best cup of coffee ever. You can stay with me forever." Touching my hand, she kissed me on the cheek. Her hand would then travel all over my body *touching those hard to reach parts.* To me, it was just another cup of coffee.

As the months went by, the morning coffee turned into a little more than just coffee. In the darkness of the morning, I decided to make a slice of toast with a little butter and a slice of cheese, mostly a sharp cheddar cheese.

Now at sunrise I was a short-order cook. I had, crafted, unintentionally, a new morning itinerary. The coffee had to go up first, and then I slipped the bread into the toaster. The butter and the cheese had to be out, as well as the two cups, one vertical and the other horizontal, ready for the sugar and coffee. When the bread popped out of the toaster, I immediately put the hard butter on the hot bread. This was done as quickly as possible. The butter needed time to melt. I had already begun to slice the cheese. By the time I finished slicing the cheese, the butter had warmed enough so I could spread it without tearing holes in the bread. The slices of cheese found their home on top of the buttered toast. Last of the preparations was the pouring of the coffee.

This meant not forgetting to put sweetener in her cup.

Adrianne was extraordinarily gracious to me after her morning coffee. I had to acknowledge this without upsetting the morning ritual. I decided to do away with the paper toweling and substituted beautifully designed napkins from Tiffany's.

Now, my delivery procedure was as follows: the toasted bread was put on top of her coffee; this I carried in my left hand with a Tiffany napkin. My toast and coffee went into my right hand with a similar napkin. A tray may have been better, but that would not feel right. I had become proficient in turning off the light with my elbow, chin, and once with my shoulder. The hallway was a breeze, now the hard part.

Slowly, I made my way up the stairs, counting the thirteen steps to the top. Halfway there, I would hear Adrianne positioning herself to receive the morning gift that had come to mean so much to her, to us, for reasons still unknown to me. She had, over time, found different ways to show me her appreciation.

Since I started the mornings romancing Adrianne with coffee in bed, I never had to worry about Adrianne having a headache, backache, or honey it's too early. All my wishes came true in the early dawn of day—of course, after the morning coffee.

Sometimes in the most ordinary of activities, there are unforeseen rewards.

Burying the Dog

In my family, it takes six people to bury a dog.

It was a very cold weekend in early March, which was preceded by the snowiest February in twenty-five years. My son decided to bury Emma, his daughter's dog, outside in the frozen tundra of upstate New York, rather than cremate Emma as he had done with his other dog, Dante, two years earlier.

The occasion, although somber, turned into a generational example of respect and responsibility you have to your animals who must be cared for in life and death. Burying Emma was a rite of passage for my nieces, nephews, and our eldest granddaughter, Bianca.

The cast of family members was, in order of importance: Emma; my brother, Dave; my son, Elwyn; his wife, Lisa; their daughter, Bianca; my wife, Arda; and me.

Dave is the oldest and the patriarch of our extended families. He is the poster image of a man and his dog. He loves dogs and they love him. He cares for them: diagnoses their illnesses, doctors them back to health, keeps them healthy, and can, when given enough time, train them to socialize with humans and other dogs. He understands them and they recognize a friend and kindred soul in him.

Dave took charge of the burial details and organized the distribution of shovels and picks needed to break through the frozen earth, the barrels to hold the earth after digging, and to make room for the body. He selected the general location for the burial site.

Elwyn carried the dog. The dog was at peace wrapped up in newly ironed bed sheets. I carried the shovels and an assortment of smaller earth working tools.

We started on the journey to the burial site. Dave did not realize how deep the snow was and had to turn back to put on his tall snow boots. The other members of the burial detail had not yet arrived. We walked to the far end of the field near the blueberry patch. By the time we reached the far end, Dave had rejoined our group. This was important as it was his land and we thought he should pick out the spot for the grave. It was known amongst family and friends if you wanted to bury your animal and stay local, talk to Dave and bring a shovel.

There was no sun out that day. It looked like 5 p.m. rather than noon. Elwyn and Dave discussed where the grave would be, and how we were going to handle the digging chores. The process seemed easy enough until we started clearing the top snow and began to dig. The basic idea was to put the earth we removed from the hole in barrels so that we could use it later to fill in the grave after we lay Emma down. It was smooth sailing for the first five minutes, and then, we hit our first level of stones, or big rocks. Rocks seemed to win out in the naming category. We now needed the three of us to get under a few of the larger rocks and leverage them out of the hole. After every rock was removed, we were able to continue the digging. The deeper we dug the bigger the rocks.

Just about this time, we could see the other members of the crew walking toward us. Bianca was helping her aunt trudge through the snow. You could tell that they too did not expect the snow to be so dense and deep. It was hard work just getting to us.

Their arrival was an occasion to stop digging and take a modest but much-needed break from the continued excavation.

Emma was a favorite of Bianca's. She grew up with the dog and, at the precious and tender age of seven, felt a great loss when Emma "passed on." Elwyn and Lisa did not like to use the word "died." Bianca wanted to help dig, but that was too dangerous, so we gave her the honor of reciting a poem when we finished placing Emma in her grave.

The grave was finally ready. Dave slowly took the dog from Elwyn and with tears in his eyes prepared to place Emma into the grave, at the same time whispering soothing words to her as he slowly lowered her body into her final resting place.

Lisa and Bianca wanted to have one last look at Emma before we covered her. When Lisa and Bianca finished saying their goodbyes, we began to fill in the grave. When that was done, we covered the earth with fresh snow and placed all the rocks we had removed from the hole on top of the grave. The stones would serve as a marker.

Bianca opened her rainbow book and began to read her poem aloud for everyone to hear and acknowledge with her the passing of her dog. Her new puppy, Mellie, and Dave's dog, Rusty, were running around us as the ceremony proceeded. It seemed fitting. With the last rock set securely in place, we gave Bianca and Lisa a hug and began to gather the tools and anything else that did not belong out in the field.

Judging by the feeling around the gravesite, I felt we accomplished something more than just burying a dog. We performed a ceremony that exemplified a caring and respect for animals that we wanted to pass on to the next generation. Leading by example matters.

As we approached the house, someone suggested that we have a shot of bourbon to finish off the morning's ceremony and, of course, hot chocolate for Bianca. We agreed this was a good idea.

The Afternoon Bike Ride

Most weekday afternoons when I return home from work, although tired, I have all sorts of grandiose plans of what to do with the rest of the day. The list is long: finish splitting wood, change the engine oil on my chain saw, read the last chapters of the *King of Thrones*, or take a midday nap. It is exhausting just thinking about the choices. Given my state of mind and its indecisiveness to make a choice, it's best to have a nap.

The cushions on my lounging chair draw me irresistibly closer. As the first shoe comes off and the soft blanket floats across the lower part of my body like the fine cashmere blanket it is, most of my thoughts of wonderful choices disappear. When the second shoe slips off, all my well-intentioned plans have gone elsewhere.

I find it best at these moments to just prop my feet up on the footstool and close the two windows to my world.

Now a most peaceful journey to nowhere begins. As I approach the point of no return on my temporary sojourn, I hear voices, voices that have followed me into my sanctuary of sleep. The voices are coming from far away, but yet I hear them. I begin to hear snippets of conversation directed at me.

"He's really getting lazy. I remember when he would be out on his bike ten minutes after getting out of his car."

"Times have changed," a voice says.

"He knows he feels better after he rides," from another.

"Why doesn't he just do it?"

"Because he's too comfortable," the other voice answers.

Slowly, very slowly my mind's eye looks around the room and observes a film crew adjusting their equipment. The director is arguing with the cameraman to get closer to me so he can film my response to their almost inaudible comments.

"Look at him, his feet propped up on the cushion. He will never get out on the bike today," the director sneered.

They continue to argue whether I will take or will not take my afternoon bike ride. Their conversation, although hushed, continues. The director is convinced that I will not ride today—for one thing, the sun is already in its downward afternoon trajectory; secondly, it's windy outside, and lastly the Newtonian theory in physics states: *Matter at rest tends to stay at rest*, which he knows from past experiences; it's a physics principle I actively practice.

The cameraman calls out: "He needs the oxygen; he needs the ride. He did not ride yesterday, that would make it two days in a row.

"Can you not see his belly getting bigger? His muscles are beginning to atrophy; his hands are beginning to shake. This amigo is a mess."

The director looks squarely at me and then turns to his crew. In a sly and mocking way, he says, "You notice he left out bike riding in his wonderful list of things to do. He's not fooling us."

And in unison they begin to chant "Slacker! Slacker!"

Enough, enough! Listening to them cackle and bemoan my character, or lack thereof, is worse than getting on my bike. I will deal with the voices later.

First, and most difficult of all I have to put my shoes back on. This always takes longer than I think it will. With that done I can hear the deafening silence in the living room. *They* are nervous, the filming has stopped. No time to ponder these events. I have to get to the garage and review my checklist for the ride. Tires are still hard, my gloves, helmet, and vest are at the ready as well. I roll the pant cuff on my right leg up two-three inches so it won't get caught in the chain. I hit the door opener and move the bike into position. A single step and I am on my way.

The exhilaration is immediate. How nice it is to turn the pedals. Slowly at first and then later in the ride the pedals turn faster and faster. By the first one hundred rotations, I complete a mental check on the physical well-being of my trusted steed of steel. All is well. Soon I will be breathing a little harder—always a good feeling.

Now, to decide which route to ride. Should I be a wuss today and take the relatively flat course or go for the hills and push this lazy body of mine? Or is it this *lazy mind* of mine? Today I shall choose the easier ride. It was hard enough just getting on the bike.

By now my joints are beginning to loosen and my breathing is more rhythmical. My cadence is higher and my heartbeats are in sync with my breathing. That combination gives my body the feeling of a well-tuned engine. Maybe I will add a hill or two on the backside; yeah, let's do that.

Somewhere along this late afternoon ride a subtle transformation has taken place. The thoughts in my mind feel less crowded. I can move them around more easily; put the non-sensical ones at the back, which will leave more room for the important stuff up front. In effect, I have rearranged the living room of my mind. I know the wind at my back, somehow, assisted me in this effort.

An hour later as I pedal up the last ten yards to the house, I feel I have defied once again, the gods of inertia. I put my accomplice of steel back in its resting place—ditto for the helmet and gloves. It's then that I began to look forward to taking my shoes off, propping my feet up on the cushion and finish what I had intended to do before *they appeared*.

As I sat there, feeling satisfied with myself, I looked around the room and out of the corner of my eye, although squinting, I can see "them" carrying out the film equipment muttering and cursing to themselves: "We'll be back, we'll be back."

They will, I know, all too soon, be back. It may even be as early as tomorrow, but certainly by the next day. *They* will never leave me.

The sun has now fallen below the horizon and I say out loud to no one in particular, "One day I am going to ask, *'What's the name of this film you're shooting in the living room of my mind?'*"

Now, it's time for my well-earned nap.

The Unexpected Mourners

The year was 2010. It was the first Sunday in September. We had a clear blue sky above, with an orange sun that took up most of it. It was unusually hot and humid for early September. Barely any wind.

But it's never a good day for a funeral. Especially when you're burying your daughter. I'd been in a daze for the past three days. Same for the rest of the family. I could easily say that anyone I knew who knew Bebe was in the same state of mind, but I could not think that much. My head could not get past the first entry—my daughter was being buried today.

We were moving very slowly. We had no place to go except to the graveyard. Thankfully, we'd been led through these days of awe by custom. The custom of preparing a body and its spirit after death that had been established in the Jewish religion thousands of years past.

I dressed in my best black suit, white shirt, and black tie. Arda looked at me and said, "Bebe would be proud of you. You look the way she would want you to look. Like her father."

At 11:00 a.m. we waited in our limousine for
the moment to walk to the gravesite. All of us
were dressed in black irrespective of the hot sun
and high humidity. This was custom; no outliers
here. Not now. The idea of Bebe not being with
us was still in the ether. Having that roadmap of
tradition to follow helped in times like these. It
sounded silly to say that Bebe was a beautiful
young woman, athletic, an organizer, a graduate
with a master's degree from UCLA— that her
annual vacations were spent volunteering with
Habitat for Humanity—that she helped build a
library in Tanzania with her mom just last year.
None of this mattered now. They were just
words. How could I tell people of the life she
lived?

As instructed by the cemetery director, we
waited for the hearse to begin its pilgrimage to the
gravesite. It felt hotter than ever, and it seemed to
me that all the cars were black even though that
was not possible. The parking lot was filled to
capacity with cars that I mostly recognized. But,
more cars kept arriving, with people inside that
I *didn't* recognize. My first impression was
another funeral was being held at the same
time. It was Sunday, always a crowded day at a
cemetery. Especially if you're Jewish. I watched
the people walk from their cars, never more
than two abreast, like a procession in a Fellini
movie, in the same direction as my family and

the other members of our funeral party. We walked in the sun, and not a sound could be heard. Maybe I was too numb to hear anything. There were very few trees, if any, along our procession.

I watched two groups of people walk in the direction of Bebe's burial site. Maybe fifty or more people were in the second group. It took me a few moments before I realized they too were going to her funeral. I didn't know them. They took their place around the gravesite and now were part of the whole—indistinguishable from Bebe's family of immediate relatives and known friends.

A limousine pulled up alongside the gravesite. An elderly man was helped out of the car. A chair was supplied for him to sit on, but the sun was too strong and he appeared to become faint. He was immediately put back into the air-conditioned limo. He lowered his window so he could hear and see the ceremony while being comfortable. A buzz went around the group that I was unfamiliar with. "It's Mr. Deutsch—he may have fainted." Mr. Deutsch was the president of the wine company that Bebe worked for. He had hired her to direct the specialty wine market the company was developing in California.

There were now close to a hundred people trying to squeeze around the immediate gravesite.

You heard the crying and saw the tears. Many people wore looks of disbelief. Bebe was young, beautiful, and pregnant when she died.

After the incantation for the newly passed, the Rabbi, who was a friend of Bebe's, spoke about her, and the comments were intimate, private, and revealing of Bebe's passion for life. The Rabbi then acknowledged all the people around her. She knew they had reason to be here, and to pay their respects to a colleague, a friend. Bebe was important in their lives.

I don't know why I was surprised by all the strange faces at the gravesite. But, I was. *Who were they?* I wondered. *How did they know Bebe? Why didn't I know them?* There were too many people here for them all to be just friends. In any case, I thought I *knew* all of Bebe's friends. We were close.

Bebe's brother and her lifelong best friend, Katherine, gave the eulogy then. It was fitting. They were of her generation.

The Rabbi next said the mourners' prayer and that was the signal to fill the grave, shovelful by shovelful. Everyone, old or young, male or female, took a turn covering Bebe's coffin with a shovelful of earth. We helped those who could not shovel for themselves until the entire coffin was covered. When the last person completed this honor of covering the coffin with earth, the Rabbi spoke of dust to dust and ashes to ashes. Finally, the Mourner's Kaddish was said, and that concluded the service.

It was very quiet at this moment. I tore my shirt, as did everyone in our family, to signify the loss of a family member. Everyone was sweating and the noonday sun was at its strongest. Yet we did not want to leave. Did not want to say goodbye to her.

I cried out to the heavens, but I didn't look up. Instead I looked down into her grave. "Bebe, how could you leave me. Why? Why Bebe? Look, Bebe, look around. Look at all your friends. We are all here for you to see." I talked to her as if she was at fault. "What are we going to do without you?"

The tears were choking me. Still, I realized I could not let this moment pass. I asked those people who were her friends, but not mine, whom I didn't know and had never met before, to stay a few moments longer and tell me who they were and how they knew Bebe.

I walked to the only tree near the gravesite along with Bebe's mom and siblings, and we greeted each friend. The line stretched for a good twenty-five yards. They understood the symbol of our wanting to meet them, so many of whom were unknown to us.

In the heat of day, unable to control my tears or sobs, unable to speak clearly, I asked each person their name and how they had come to know Bebe. They too could not hold back their tears; many hugged her mom and then me. They too found it difficult to speak even the simplest condolences.

I tried hard, between our mutual and collective sobs, to listen and remember their names and the details they shared. I did recognize some of her school friends, and I did recognize names of people that Bebe worked with, but I hadn't met them before today. I saw her high school prom date, Ossama, of twenty years ago. How had he known of Bebe's passing? And so on. Her friends from elementary school, through high school, and then into college years were all there. I remembered many of them when they spoke their names.

Her business friends were all new to me. They came from France, Italy, California, Spain, Chile, and other locations where wine was important to the economy. Vintners, importers, industry reporters from faraway places were here to pay their last respects to our daughter. I didn't know she had had so many friends. I held onto to each of them, known or unknown to me, a little longer than was necessary. I gave up trying to dry my eyes and face.

It seemed that I, we, the immediate family, were supposed to leave first, followed by the others. We could not leave. Not yet. I invited every person I met at the tree to come to our home, Bebe's home, and visit. There was food and drink for all, I said. In truth, I simply hoped that they would come and share more stories of their friendship with Bebe. I somehow had missed so much of her life and wanted to fill in the blanks.

"Somewhere over the rainbow way up high and the dreams that you dream of, once in a lullaby. Someday I'll wish upon a star and see you standing there."

These words were put on her footstone for all to read.

A Hard Look in the Mirror

The difference between dreams and reality.

Finally, a parking lot close to my office. The scarcity of parking space in New York City is now a common experience for most people who still drove into the city for work. Although it was an uncovered lot, hot in the summer and cold in the winter, distance, price, and availability mattered. This would be the living quarters for my five-year-old Volvo in the foreseeable future.

At the end of the block, parked on the corner of the street, was a sixteen foot van with a low back and a sliding overhead door. It was old. Most of the white paint had peeled off a long time ago. Rust spots were everywhere. The last block of unblemished white paint was covered with "Kappy Fruit." Somebody left off the possessives from the sign. On the sidewalk side of the truck was a homemade wooden fruit and vegetable stand filled with produce. I was surprised how many different fruits and vegetables were on display. All the basics as well as a few specialty vegetables for his Caribbean and Latin American customers.

I normally parked my car in the lot a little before ten each day. By this time there was a line of customers, mostly women, all waiting to buy their fruits and vegetables. Having three children of my own who eat as much fruit as I can buy, the evening trip back to the parking lot included a trip to Kappy's fruit truck. For the first six months I would line up like everyone else, buy my three pounds of bananas for a dollar and three pounds of apples for another dollar, along with oranges, grapefruit, tomatoes, and any specialty imports that Kappy had on his stand. I bought a lot of stuff. He presented whatever fruit and vegetables were in season as well as the specialty foods that reminded his customers of their distant homeland.

As weeks went by, I began to appreciate his business ability and his hard work—a retired postal worker who somehow found his way to a food truck, a corner, and a successful business—always wearing the same flat cap every day whose original color was now unrecognizable; it had long ago faded into a dirty-street grey. That, along with his signature rust-colored three-quarter jacket, made Kappy stand out "from the madding crowd." His customers loved him. Besides buying fresh, you had to love him just for that, he would, many times, extend credit to his customers. "Pay you payday," they would call out as they closed their shopping bags and went back to work.

Soon, I graduated from buying loose fruits to buying cases. Kappy always offered a better price if you bought a case. For cases, he had to go back into the truck and pull out what you wanted. It reminded me of old New York gangster movies—of "getting something special" from the back of the truck.

Without fanfare or notice, another produce vendor parked right next to Kappy's truck. Now he had to get to his parking spot a little earlier than before just to secure his space and be first off the corner. Competition was not friendly. The new kid on the block was jealous of Kappy's customers.

One day, as I prepared to pick up my car, I had a phone message from Arda, my wife, to pick up a case of pink grapefruit: Kappy's truck was not there. This usually meant his truck broke down or he broke down. So I got in line to buy some grapefruit from the new guy. I was next in line and he recognized me as one of Kappy's customers. He said as loud as he could, "I am not serving you, I see you only when Kappy is not here." Embarrassed, but not showing it, I left the line. Things were territorial and personal. Buying fruit was not easy on the corner of 26th Street.

Kappy did not resent the competition. He had, in his own way, been around the block; he was easy to get along with. I was curious about his business. On very cold days of winter, I would buy Kappy a cup of coffee. Ten a.m. was a quiet time sandwiched between the morning rush and the afternoon lunch hour. It was a good time to talk about the fruit business. I did the listening. Over time, I was able to put together the daily routine of how he managed his business.

Kappy lived in Queens and left his house by 2 a.m. every morning. He would drive to Hunt's Point Food Market in the Bronx and pick up the daily selection of fruits and vegetables. Most mornings he would arrive at the corner of 26th street by 7:30. He finished each day at 6:00 p.m. and was off the corner by 6:30. He kept this schedule from Monday through Friday. He did not work Saturday or Sunday.

Late one afternoon in July, as he was packing up for the day, I noticed he had a lot of perishable fruit still left on his truck. "Kappy," I said, "what do you do with the fruit that is about to spoil, like the melons." He smiled, "You need a few restaurants that will buy your overripe produce. Twice a week I stop at restaurants that I know will take the unsalable produce."

He continued, "I cover my costs and don't have to throw any stuff away. It's the only way to control my products and continue to sell fresh."

He had it all figured out. He and a helper managed the fruit stand, bought fresh, sold fresh and moved out the near spoiled and blemished produce. He paid for all goods and services in cash and was likewise paid in cash. Kappy liked telling me about his cash business. "You seem awfully interested in this business. Maybe you would like to operate your own fruit truck?" He asked.

I was interested, and I was pleasantly surprised that he would bring up the subject. I had been thinking about just that: operating a fruit truck on a street corner in Manhattan. Everything about the business appealed to me. A five-day week business, one employee, maybe none at the beginning and most attractive, a cash business. It all sounded very promising. "Mr. Harvey," he began, "I can get you the truck. I can establish credit for you with the wholesalers that I deal with and, most importantly, I get you a corner a block from here." It sounded too good to be true. "How much money a year are we talking about?" I asked. He smiled and said, "I make, in a bad year, a minimum of a 100k. I know you like the business. It would be nice having you on the next corner, just in case I run out of goods or need help with a flat." He laughed, knowing this would never happen.

The drive home was bizarre. I fantasized about driving my truck to my corner and setting up my fruit stand, making my first sale and my first thousand.

I told Arda about my conversation with Kappy and she too was excited. Home on the weekend, cash, healthy outdoor work, just had to worry about snow days. The following day I drove into Manhattan and parked a little before 7 a.m. I wanted to see the action from the beginning of the day until the end. Kappy knew exactly what I was doing. "So," he said, "what do you think about my proposal?"

"I accept," I responded. He offered to let me work a few days on the truck. "That would be ideal. It would answer all my questions about the venture."

He suggested that I meet him at the food market. "Sure," I responded.

"Let's do Tuesday, Wednesday, and Thursday. Meet me at Hunt's point at 3:30 a.m., at the entrance to the market. I will show you where to park and then you can jump into the truck and that is where we'll begin."

He was wrong. I began when I got up at midnight. It felt as if I just fallen asleep. It took twenty-five minutes to get dressed in the appropriate winter clothing. I left the house at two. It took fifty minutes to get there.

The coffee truck at the entrance to the market was a welcome sight. I was early, so I had plenty of time to enjoy my first cup of what

70

would be many cups that day. Kappy arrived at 3:30 a.m. sharp. I had figured out the parking logistics and was ready to jump into the truck as Kappy pulled up. We finished loading by 5:30, which included 130 cases of fruits and vegetables. We bought the produce from three different distributors. I was tired, but I knew we would have to unload most of the cases we had in the truck. The setup was ok; we were street ready by 7:30 a.m. As we finished, the first customer stepped up to the pushcart. Ten hours later we repacked the cases that were out of the truck, including the loose produce.

We drove back to Hunt's Point. I picked up my car and drove home. Kappy drove the truck to Queens and parked it in his garage. I pulled my car into my garage a little before 9 p.m. I remember kicking my boots off and falling on the bed. That was all.

Arda woke me at midnight and my day started all over. I was more efficient with my time and realized I could get up at 12:45 a.m. and still get to the market at 3:00 a.m. This was Wednesday. We repeated the same process as the morning before. We had fewer cases to load, but business had been good so we knew tomorrow would be another heavy morning. Nothing of consequence changed during the day. We finished at 6 p.m. and got to Hunt's point at 7:30. I pulled into my garage a little before 9:00. Passed out on the bed with my boots on.

The next morning, it took Arda a little longer to wake me than the night before. Even so, I was at the market at 3 a.m. I jumped into Kappy's truck and promptly fell asleep. I slept every chance I had. At the corner, I unpacked the cases of fruit and vegetables.

Ten hours later, I packed up and loaded the truck. Slept all the way to the Hunt's point market. Jumped into my car and drove about twenty minutes before I pulled into an all-night 7-Eleven. I parked and went to sleep, couldn't make the trip home without catching some shut eye. I don't remember what time I pulled into the garage, but I do remember, sleeping with my boots on.

Arda woke me at 12:45 but I could not get up. At 3:30 Kappy called to find out what happened to me. "Overslept," I said. "See you at the corner." I took a shower, the first in three days. I arrived at the corner a few minutes before 8 a.m. It was too late; Kappy had already unloaded and set up the cart. He looked at me and we both burst out laughing. We knew this would not work for me. A close look in the mirror revealed the truth: "This was too hard for me," even though Kappy paid me a thousand dollars for the three days I worked with him.

It was difficult for me to accept the unvarnished truth that my distance from the market and then to the street corner was simply too far. The workday was simply too long to give me the rest I needed to make this work.

At a closer "look in the mirror," I realized I had turned down a six-figure income because it left me exhausted with no time for my family. I was not hungry enough to sacrifice my family, not for the root of all evil. I actually had limitations. Kappy understood the sacrifice I was not willing to make.

We never spoke again about setting up a separate fruit truck operation in Manhattan. A few years later, I moved my import business out of the city and settled in upstate New York. Soon after, Kappy closed down the fruit business and moved to Arizona with all his money and memories.

My Friend Mr. Knowles

Shortly after I started my own business, selling fashionable, fabric-covered blank books, I found myself in the frightening position of being one of *those* people. A person that doesn't belong. There, in the back corner of a Hallmark store on 3rd Avenue and 63rd Street, my tie never straight, briefcase in hand, my white shirt stained with sweat, I stood, hoping to see whoever was in charge.

A man I felt sure was the owner/manager was in the front of the store, standing on a raised platform. From his position, he clearly saw everyone and everything that went on in the store during the busy lunch hour. Barely glancing in my direction, he motioned for me to come to him. The elevated platform allowed him to look straight down at me without bending over. He silently gestured for me to come closer. It strained my neck to look up at him. All I saw were his pince-nez glasses and unshaven chin.

"What are you selling? Don't you know better than to come in at lunchtime, our busiest time? I shouldn't, but I'll give you a few minutes. Show me what you got."

My hands began to shake as I took out my beautifully covered blank diaries and art journals. Each book was covered in imported Marrimeko designed fabrics from Finland. The diaries and journals were hand bound using the finest glues and binding material then available.

"Whoa, not all at once. Put them back in your case and show me what you have *one at a time.*"

I handed him my best-styled books first— one at a time—then watched his smile turn into a smirk and then into a scowl.

"Is this what you're selling? A blank book? No lines? This is a piece of shit. Show me the next."

I did, and then the next. After each presentation, he would say "shit, shit, shit."

Never did I look up as I handed him book after book. There were many samples to show. Finally, I finished my presentation and began putting my samples back in their case. The man above me waited until I had closed my case so he would have my undivided attention.

"I'll give you some friendly, free advice. You look like a nice young man. Get out of this business. Nothing you showed me has a chance of selling in a Hallmark store. You're wasting your time. Go back to school, marry a school-teacher—and straighten your tie."

Looking back on the moment, I remember well how I fought back tears, barely mumbled, "Thank you for your time," and left the store. Stumbling along, I felt I had been whipped, pussy whipped and pistol-whipped. I didn't wear a tie for the next two years.

Still, time passed, and I did sell my diaries and art journals. In fact, within three years I had moved from selling store to store on the streets of Manhattan to attending national trade shows specifically tailored to the stationary and gift industry.

It was the third day of the Spring Trade show, the show where store buyers placed orders for the upcoming Christmas season.

Standing and looking at my display of fancy, covered art journals was the same stationary store owner who had given me his "friendly, *free*" advice: *Get out of the stationary business, go back to school and marry a schoolteacher.*

He was the devil in my dreams. I moved closer to see the incisors that dripped sulfuric acid on my fabric covers and ate holes through stacks of my books. Where was his pale and ghostlike complexion? He looked normal standing in my booth. He did not recognize me, but I recognized him. Surely, after answering his questions about waterproof fabrics and the modern day marvel of Scotchgard, he would remember, if not me, the fancy covered blank books that were displayed throughout the booth. I waited and waited for the scowl to appear as it had three years ago.

"Mr. Knowles," his name, Myron Knowles, was on the show badge, "please sit down. I will hand you the books *one at a time* so that you may choose the best designs for your Christmas windows," I said. My tone was casual, but firm.

"I like that," he said, "It gives me time to get the essence of each design."

"An excellent choice of words—the essence of each design," I parroted. I was certain he would recognize his own demand that I submit each fabric book *one at a time* and that this would be the *aha* moment.

But no, nothing. He ordered quite a lot of books. We discussed payment and shipping terms. And I was still sure he would remember me. *But he did not.* Only I remembered.

When he left the booth and was safely down the aisle, I tore up his order and threw it in the wastebasket. No good sense in having those memories bubble up and percolate in my mind. *Out of sight out of mind.* Thankfully, the trade show confrontation was a memory that did not linger. I was too busy filling existing orders and expanding my wares. Over the next year my line of blank art books grew to incorporate cooking journals, telephone address books, scrapbooks, and composition books.

The following spring arrived quickly. I prepared for the annual trade show, this time with many more products to display.

It was again on the third day of the show that Mr. Knowles walked into my booth. He did not look happy. I was sure this time that he remembered me and was going to tell me what a mistake he had made by ordering from me, and since I had not shipped his order to please cancel it. "Cancel it in writing!" he would say. However, that's not what happened.

"Where's my order from last year? I spent a lot of time selecting the journals and sketch pads for my Christmas display. What happened? Did my credit not check out? If so, you should've called me! Will you ship my order for *this* Christmas season?" he inquired. His voice was now an octave higher than when he had begun speaking, near screaming.

Never having expected to see him again, I now found myself in a dilemma. Should I keep up the facade and assure him that this time his order would be shipped? Alternatively, should I tell him what I had done with his order and face the consequences? My interest in finding out *his* side of the story motivated me to tell Mr. Knowles of our first meeting three years ago.

"Mr. Knowles, I was in your store three years ago and I showed you books and journals very similar to those you ordered at the last show. Your response to me, after disparaging my book designs, was 'go back to school and marry a school teacher.'

"I actually cried when I left your store. I swore I would find a way to get even with you, but I soon forgot because I was actually too busy growing my business. Then you walked into my booth last spring and ordered my books—the same ones you said would never sell in a Hallmark store. From the beginning of writing your order I had no intention of shipping it. I ripped it up into little pieces."

Mr. Knowles took my hand and quietly said, "I'm so sorry, I don't remember anything about our meeting. It must've been the week I found out my life partner, and business partner, was diagnosed HIV positive. Others have told me of the nasty things I said and did that week. The news filled me with unimaginable grief and despair. I am truly sorry, and I am so glad that you did not listen to me."

As he was speaking, his partner who by this time apparently could not understand what was taking Myron so long, came looking for him. Myron grabbed his partner by the arm and began telling him my story, our story, all over again.

"This kid," he said to his partner, "has a big pair of balls. In addition, he is smart. He ripped up my order and said 'fuck you' to me! Imagine that."

Mr. Knowles turned to me and again said, "I'm truly, truly sorry."

He fumbled for something in his briefcase and pulled out a small tin of Beluga caviar.

"Here," he said, "take this tin of caviar; it's the best quality and quite expensive. I hope this makes up for what I did, and I really like your books. Will you ship them this season?"

Three years of nightmares and self-doubt vanished in an instant, and a budding friendship grew in its place.

"Yes. I will ship the order."

Knowles and I remained friends for a number of years thereafter. I filled all his orders from that point on. He would, on occasion, hand me a tin of Beluga caviar as a sign of remembrance of our journey together. We met at a time of sadness with a healthy dose of vitriol. Somehow, strangely, this became a compound for a lasting friendship.

He and his partner both died of AIDS in the late 80s.

The Dance

You've watched her all night. You know she knows she's the best dancer on the floor. Her tight red dress, flaring out from the waist down is the perfect contra-point to her three-inch open-toed dance shoes. Red of course. She is the reason you are here tonight.

However, first you must catch her attention. She has many admirers. All the best dancers want to dance with her. She is known around the Argentine dance halls as the "rojo flor" (red flower). The night is passing and still no contact.

Finally, after many attempts, she has caught your facial gesture and acknowledged your request. Yes! She has accepted your invitation to dance.

Be bold! Walk slowly to meet her. The music has not yet started. Don't be nervous; say something short and sweet. She is smiling.

"Olah Señorita, habla Anglais?" you ask.

"Yes, I speak English," she answers.

She moves closer to you. Her perfume is intoxicating. You can feel your hands begin to shake. Luckily, the music begins.

Don't rush. You have time. Let her hear the music, watch her eyes, her hands; is she ready and willing to dance to the heavens with you?

Slowly, you extend your hand. Slowly, she places her hand in yours. You ever so gently close your fingers around hers and gently place your arm around her bare shoulders. Her skin is warm to the touch. Her long hair covers the fingers of your right hand.

She places her breasts against your chest The pressure is titillating. You could stay with her for the rest of your life. But, that is not your mission. You have offered her the gateway to paradise. Now dance.

The floor is impossibly crowded. It is 2 a.m. No room on any side of you, but she does not care. She has placed her trust in you. Do not disappoint! Dance! She squeezes you hard around the chest, in beat with the music. You are overwhelmed with emotion.

Don't pass out. Dance! Dance!

The music has fully energized your senses. You step slowly, longly, to your left, making sure you have changed her weight; so that her right foot is free to take the step with you. She feels your command through your chest and moves with you as one.

Violins take hold of you with their melodic, smooth interpretation; speaking to the bandellions. The measure of four makes you comfortable. You are in familiar territory. Walk,

walk, never break the connection. Let the thrust of your pelvis guide your partner. Stand erect!

Her eyes are closed. She has given herself to you. Do not fail.

Sense where the trouble will come from; don't rush! Move like a cat; keep breathing, no undo pressure. All forward movement is closed off to you. You must dance in a small circle. A circle you can protect with your body. She must know nothing of the impending doom around her.

Gently she squeezes your hand as if to give you courage to move forward. Stay calm, you can dance your way to freedom. Be bold!

You take a long step to the right; she comes with you. All her weight is now on her left foot. You step back, slightly. This lets her lean forward onto your chest. She understands the movement. You feel the acceleration of her heartbeat.

She is amongst the stars. Keep her there. The music has now taken over the dance. The instruments are talking to each other. Faster, louder, they keep pounding the beat. The dancers feed off the music, and the musicians feed off the dancers. The dance floor is undulating to the beat of the base violins. She hears and feels, but does not break the bond between the two.

Your steps are stronger. Yet still smooth. You turn with her and move along the edges of the dance floor. She senses the change in tempo. She responds with you. A shorter step a quicker pivot. Her heart is beating faster. You tell yourself to breathe, or else you will faint. Her cheek is pressed against yours. Eyes still shut. You know she has left this place on earth and traveled elsewhere. She will never tell you where, and you dare not ask.

You have, unknowingly, moved into a zone on the floor that is less crowded. You look around and see all the better dancers enjoying this moment of freedom. For soon, it will disappear. Dance now to impress while you have the space.

As you shift her weight onto her right foot, you again gently step back so that she has the sensation of falling slightly forward, while still being supported by your chest. You walk around her keeping her on one foot. With her free foot, she begins to play with your leg, moving her foot seductively up and down your leg. Slowly she wraps her foot around your hip. At this moment, you place your weight to imperceptibly collide with her leg and wait for her leg to ricochet off in a big round flourish. Little movement, big result. Slowly, always slowly, you guide her back to both feet. You pause, no movement, motionless. You hold her a little tighter. Slowly you guide her weight from one foot to the other. It is like rocking a cradle.

You think only of the woman in your arms. You must soon let her go. But, maybe she will agree to another dance with you. Dare you ask? She opens her eyes and smiles at you. Whispering, "That was beautiful."

You ask, "Un otro?" (Another?)

She responds, "Por supuesto." (Of course)

You both smile. You talk to each other without speaking. Each anxious to get back to the moment when the heavens opened up on earth. To continue the dance of love.

Tango in the Beginning

I waited, with Arda, at the actors' exit door hoping to talk with Carols Gavito, the star of the Broadway show, "Tango Argentine." Luckily, for me, he was one of the first to leave the theatre.

"Senor Gavito, por favor, I loved your dance performance and would like to take lessons from you. Do you teach beginners?" I hurriedly asked him as he walked out the door.

"No, I do not teach beginners!" he said. "You must go around the corner and take lessons at the Tango studio on 57th Street," and with that, he continued on his way.

The following week, we joined the chaos of a hundred people in a dance class on 57th Street trying to learn the Argentine Tango. The experience was humbling and impossible. I parked the thought of learning the Tango in the far recesses of my mind.

This was in the early 90s. I was unaware the Broadway show had created a small group of dedicated aficionados to promote and dance the tango in New York City. It very quickly became the center of tango in the USA.

Three years later, on a late fall night, Arda and I went to see "Evita," the movie. The theater was crowded, and we sat in the front, which we never do. I don't like to look up. In the movie there was a dance scene following Eva Peron's funeral. I wasn't sure, but I think I counted ten couples dancing the Tango. Having seen the Broadway show, we recognized the dance immediately. The dancers were in their 30s and 40s. Not too young. To me, they danced the way I imagined I wanted to dance.

The scene was filmed in a cafeteria with grey concrete pillars holding up the floor above. The dancers danced in a counter clockwise direction and used the pillars as props to dance around. Light came in through dirty windows spaced ten feet apart and the same height off the floor. No additional lighting was employed. The scene reflected the hard times Argentina was about to experience. Grey, without color.

It was handkerchief time for me. The music, the dancers, the somber mood that Eva's funeral created was over the top. However, I realized even then, it was always the music.

The men wore double-breasted suits, most wore hats, those who did not had slick black hair or a full head of grey hair. The men reminded me of the "Boys from Borsalino," Alain

Delon and Jean-Paul Belmondo walking the street of Marseilles. Dressed in black with their fedoras pulled down and tilted, making it hard to see their eyes. They walked with a swagger exhibiting an aura of panache and mystery. It was their street dance, *their* Tango. Fifty years later, their *mien* appeared on screen before my eyes.

The women wore evening clothes. Not formal, just dressy. Their hair black and short, cut into what appeared to be geometric angles, Latina in look. Three-inch heels, black lace nylons to match their shoes, always red lipstick. Their bodies perfectly pressed up against their man, their partners, the leaders of the dance.

The dancers were not synchronized. The movements were different for each couple. Yet, there was unity in their dance. Unrehearsed, the dancers listened to the music for their instructions. It appeared, one would think, each couple had received a unique set of instructions on how to interpret the music for their style.

No smile, the music was slow and soft. The women had their eyes closed, or so it seemed. I had to remember I was watching a film. The mood was haunting in an inspirational way.

The amalgam of passion, movement and skill, all performed to music that highlighted the Bandoneon, the instrument that became synonymous with the tango.

The dancers, without knowing it, presented that *machismo,* so famous in their culture, into their dance.

I suspected there were other places in Buenos Aires where Eva Peron's funeral was also solemnized with couples dancing the tango.

A half century of my life had passed, and it took a Broadway play and a funeral scene from a movie to experience the epiphany that changed my destiny. There, looking up at the screen, was the dance I had been unknowingly searching for all my life.

Arda and I did not speak until we reached the car. In the privacy of the car, she turned to me and asked, "Do you want to go to Argentina?"

"You read my mind. I'll look on the internet to see if there are any groups going to Buenos Aires to learn and to dance the Tango."

"Do it tonight!" she said.

Surprised, I realized there were two crazy people in the car.

* * *

Finally, in late January, I found a company in Boston that organized tango tours to Buenos Aires. Their next tour was in late March.

I spoke with the tour leader, Daniel, and made reservations for his March tour. Daniel had a wealth of information about the tango and Buenos Aires. He spoke Spanish fluently, he was an accomplished Tango instructor, sold tango CD's and arranged workshops all over the USA. He insisted that we take as many lessons in the tango as possible before going to BA. I told him we were accomplished ballroom dancers, but that did not impress him. "Call this woman in New York and take lessons with her. She was my partner for three years and she's a good teacher; and learn some Spanish idioms if you can."

He gave me a general idea of what the tour would consist of. The hotel, was located in the center of Buenos Aires. Three workshops a day, dancing every night at different ballrooms, and private parties at his cupola in downtown BA. He made it sound so pleasant, even enjoyable.

I called the instructor in NYC and arranged for two lessons a week for the next five weeks. I wanted more, but she was busy at this time of the year. After a few lessons in New York, Arda and I began to understand how difficult it was going to be to learn the tango. It was a new language.

We arrived in Buenos Aires the evening before the tour began. An immediate problem was getting the taxi driver to understand where we wanted to go. The city had not yet adopted English as its second language and we did not speak Spanish. The Hotel Lafayette was, at best, a three star, although it advertised itself as four stars.

The following morning Daniel met our group of thirty in the hotel lobby. He gave us our ten-day schedule. Three workshops a day, interspersed throughout the afternoon, each ninety minutes long.

The classes turned out to be very profound and intensely chaotic. Few of the instructors spoke English. Daniel had to interpret the lesson for us. We had so many questions, which under the circumstances, could not be answered.

Frustration and anxiety fell heavily on the *beginners*. The *beginners* group had leaders (male), and followers (female). The leaders had the almost impossible task of learning the figure, leading his partner and then dancing with her in time with the music. All in ninety minutes. We did not have time to express our frustration; there were movements to learn. I could not help Arda. I had to learn too much too quickly.

As a group, the women were completely overwhelmed. The leaders in the beginners group were too inexperienced to lead. For the women it was a never-ending cycle of disappointment and doubt: not young enough, not pretty enough, maybe a little overweight, not enough Spanish in their quiver and too few capable leaders.

The bus to take us to the milonga (dance) would leave the hotel every evening at 11 p.m. The milongas lasted until sun up. It was there that all our inadequacies were exposed. The futility of our daily labors was apparent for all to see. At the milonga most of us sat. If you were lucky, you had the option of asking a woman to dance. After one tanda (three songs), you were directed off the floor so as not to interfere with the people who could dance. Each dance venue was jammed. There never seemed to be enough room.

The recurring thought in my mind, and I guess in others as well, was what are we doing here? It was an impossible undertaking. The workshops were a blur. We went to one after another, not knowing if we learned anything. We had very little to show for our effort. Very little.

Every night at the milonga, we saw people who danced the tango. So it *was* possible, just not for *us* at this moment.

Tango was a call to arms. It would justify my existence. This was not an existential dilemma. The music had found a way into my soul. And, in order to become one with the music, I had to learn this dance.

My world was reduced to a song and a dance. All my attention was diverted to this endeavor. Time was running out! All my other interests: family, friends, obligations, all disappeared. Only the tango remained. Was I alone in this new universe? Would Arda be with me?

The enormity of the task, when not depressing me, made me laugh. What else could I do but laugh? The music made me cry, the beauty of the dance made me cry. I was overwhelmed.

Buenos Aires was the mother's milk in the tango world. It began and ended there. Everywhere else was a waiting lounge until you returned to Buenos Aires. It was there that you could dance tango morning, noon, and night. The music was born there. You were a better dancer just by being there. It was in the air, on the radio, in homes, and in nursing homes. I didn't know it, but in a little more than a week's time my life had changed.

I envied anyone in our group who already knew how to dance, even a little. I socialized with the beginners. There were quite a few of us, more women than men, as is always the case. Those in the group who could dance had nothing to do with us. We were left to the mercy of the assistants Daniel had hired to dance and partner with us, the *beginners*! The ratio of women to men portended the problems to come.

Women at the milonga had a hard time. They sat longingly, waiting to be asked to dance. They knew it keeps them younger in body and spirit. All they needed was a couple of tanda's, to be touched and held, to music that tears at their soul.

Arda was as serious as serious could be. Her feet hurt, she was tired, and she did not have much to show for it. Too few dances. I was no help. It would be the blind leading the blind. I was looking for my own lifeline to help me learn the tango. We were together, but separate. I could not save her and she knew it. Every evening Arda would do her hair, dress to kill, only to sit, occasionally dance, and watch others dance. This tour was emotionally brutal to her ID.

It was in the early morning of the eighth day when our bus pulled up to the hotel at 3 a.m. and disgorged its weary cargo into the bar. Over a glass of wine, on that night, Arda turned to me and said, "I can't do this anymore! I am not learning. I am frustrated and angry. We have two choices: one is to pack up and go home. The other is to take as many private lessons as we can before we leave."

I agreed. We needed more practice with a partner who could teach and dance. Sadly, we came to this conclusion with only three days left on the tour. The third evening, we would fly back to the USA.

We arranged to take lessons separately. I chose to learn with a female instructor and Arda arranged her lessons with an instructor who had taught two of our workshops. He was the only teacher who spoke English.

Coincidentally, he, Carlos, used the same cafeteria that appeared in "Evita" as his Sunday morning studio. The cafeteria did not open until noon for business. As in the movie, the cafeteria had no artificial lighting. The light from the windows, high off the floor, was the only light in the room. The windows were dirty, and it transformed the sunny morning into a grey, hazy setting. The dust in the air refracted the beams of light that came through the windows.

He greeted us, "Buenos dias, it is not too hot in here now. It is a good morning for learning the tango. Arda, do you have any special music or orchestra that you would like to dance to this morning?"

"No, play what you like."

"I like DiSarle, okay?"

"Perfecto," she said.

Not wanting to be intrusive in any manner, I sat at the other end of the dance floor. I heard the music, but I could only follow their shadows as they danced.

It was apparent to me, as I watched her and Carlos dance, that there was very little instruction in their movements. They were just dancing. I could sense Arda's excitement to be dancing, at last.

After ten days of great effort, and many frustrating moments, she was dancing! I watched for an hour as Arda, I believe, fell in love, passionately, with the tango, and with Carlos, who embraced her and danced her to the stars. She was elegant, confident, and more radiant than I had ever seen her.

Tears just started to flow down my cheeks. I was not crying, no sobs, no sounds, just tears. Tears of happiness, of accomplishment and pride. Standing in her three-inch high heels, she looked as if she had danced for years. I was so proud of her.

That gave me hope that I would, could, dance and lead the way Carlos did, no matter how long it takes.

"Arda, you danced very well today. It was a pleasure to dance with you."

"Gracias," she said, her cheeks turning a warm color of red.

She later told me, "I could feel the blood moving through my body; little molecules were rushing about to catch up with the music that entered into me. I have never had an experience like this before.

I smiled; our journey had begun.

The Tango House

"Where are you from?" he asked. This question has come up many times before. It could be a preamble to a nice friendly conversation, or not. I thought about the question, but before I had a chance to answer, he continued; "It's obvious that you are a foreigner. A 'Gringo'. You must come from somewhere else," he said, laughing.

He continued, "You are here to learn to dance the Tango, no? From my experiences, I would say you are from New York. I have heard this accent before. Strangely, most of the people I have met from the USA have been from New York."

"You are correct," I answered.

"Well senor, today is your lucky day. Javier and I will demonstrate how the 'close embrace' style should be danced. Watch carefully." He grinned like Felix the cat before eating his mouse. "My name is Matin. What is your name?" he asked.

"Herve."

I have met quite a few "Matins" in Argentina over the years. Their names may be different, but they are all the same. Older, retired pensioners, who frequent the dance halls that have early evening dances—sometimes, as early as 5:00 p.m. They smell from Old Spice aftershave, or Old Spice cologne. They appear slightly bent, obsequious, wearing ill-fitted trousers and a sport coat that is too long. It fit them at a younger age when they stood without stooping. I remember their teeth were imperfect and slightly yellow. They were, however, always clean-shaven—always with a pocket-handkerchief.

The "Matin's" sat in the men's section of the dance floor looking across the hall selecting, carefully, their next partner. A lonely woman, a foreigner, with a look of *please ask me to dance* pasted on her face.

Now, again, I sat next to "Matin" in Marta's Tango House. Javier, rarely spoke to me nor, or so it seemed, to anybody else. He left it up to Matin to express his annoyance and anger toward the interlopers from outside their country, with particular ire toward the "know-it-all" Americans.

Why not? His president pegged the Argentine peso to the dollar on a one-to-one basis. One dollar exchanged for one peso. It took but four years to drive the country into bankruptcy and a severe depression that they still feel today. It was easy to understand why Matin did not like me.

Now, he sees me stealing his culture and his women. It is a wonder why the "Matins" did not shoot me, or my kind.

Nevertheless, there we were sitting side by side in Marta's Tango House.

Matin now had the opportunity to show the *foreigner*, the *American,* how to dance—his dance.

Ay, Matin picked the wrong "Gringo" to mess with. You pompous son of a bitch, I thought.

"Good, it is important to keep on learning— especially from dancers who grew up in Buenos Aires and who have been dancing the tango all their lives." I said.

"Bien, bien," he said. "The Senora's living room is perfect for dancing. The granite floors allow you to pivot and move smoothly over its surface. And, there are no cracks in her floor."

I was early to the afternoon festivities. In fact, at this moment, there were only the three of us in the room. This would change. Within the half hour, the living room was full. As usual, there were always more women.

The Senora's Tango house was fully rented. Of her eight rooms, only two, had their own bathroom and shower; all other guests shared the remaining three bathrooms. The kitchen, the living room, and the outdoor patio were communal. She may have had twelve or thirteen people staying with her at this time. It was high season for tango lovers. She charged by the room amenities and by the day. Others in the living room and I were here before. The common thread, of course, was our love for the tango.

Her house was close to many of the popular dance halls. Besides, she drove a car, and went out dancing three or four times a week. If you were early enough, she would give you a lift. However, never on the weekend,

"Too crowded with tourists," she said.

I always found that odd as she had a house full of tourists.

The afternoon festivities were beginning.

The living room in the early afternoon at the senora's house was reserved for guests who had arranged for private lessons. They used the living room as a studio; this saved them the cost of a rental at a dance studio. This courtesy alone made it worth staying at Marta's.

Matin and Javier were familiar with the women in the house. They had been to Marta's Saturday dance before. The few women who were not from Buenos Aires had been living in the tango house for quite some time

Both men were retired and lived on a small pension from the state. They needed money to go out dancing, to dress up, to impress. Not having witnessed men using women to fund their evening's entertainment before, I found it unusual, but not unreasonable. The women were desperate. They had traveled at great expense to come to Buenos Aires and not being young or competent in the Tango, could sit for an evening without a dance. The savvy women recognized that a $50.00 bill solved their evening's problem. It bought their "Matin" a laundered shirt, possibly a tie, and a pair of shined shoes. She picked up the tab for the refreshments as well. However, she had a partner for the evening. She was protective of her investment. He rarely danced with another woman without first asking permission.

Matin had two endeavors: one, was to dance with the young, pretty woman that sat directly across the room, the other was to impress me. Accomplishing one without the other would not be a fulfilling afternoon for him. We both understood that.

When you sit, you watch. You learn to pay attention to the female dancers on the floor. You want to evaluate their level of proficiency. A good leader does not dance *above* the level of his partner.

Matin never learned to adjust his dance style to accommodate his partner. (He could get all the dances he wanted.) He knew just enough. I paid careful attention to his style. It was old fashioned. He held his partner too tightly; he led with his hands and his arms as if he were driving a bus and he had little variety in his figures, and he danced on his heels. The latter habit pulled his partner off balance. Always.

He was sweating when he finished his dance. An indication he had worked too hard. You should be calm and cool.

I am competitive and possibly a little too harsh in my judgment. His partner, I am sure, enjoyed every moment.

Javier was next. He was less secure than Matin, which made him less aggressive. His partner enjoyed the extra freedom of movement "to breathe." However, his style was similar to Matin's. Javier was not sweating; he was not at war with me.

I congratulated Matin on his floor craft and knowledge of the Tango.

"Eso es, (that's it) bien, bien," I said.

He did not respond, nor did he take his seat on the couch next to Javier. Instead, he and Javier went onto the patio to get a glass of wine. Surprisingly, he quickly returned and sat down next to me.

"Well, Herve, what do you think of our dance?" He wanted to say "his dance." Before I could respond, it was my turn to take the floor.

I did not ask the youngest, or prettiest—they had already danced. I chose another. A little older, more conservative in her dress. Her heel size was modest. She recognized the informality of a Saturday afternoon get together.

"May I have this dance?"

She smiled and said, "Of course."

"My name is Herve."

"And mine is Bianca."

We smiled as I offered my hand to assist her onto the floor. She accepted.

As it happens, the next series of tangos were by my favorite orchestra.

"I like Rodrigues's music very much," she said.

"I, as well. He keeps a wonderful beat and his violin arrangements of the melody are a pleasure to dance to. I am sad when I have to sit out a tanda (3 songs, in succession) of his music."

"It is the same with me," she said.

Bianca slipped easily into my arms. She knew she was going to have good dances with me. The music quickly became our third partner. She was light on her feet and sensitive to the music. Her body was mine to control as it should be. We danced to the music, and as they say, "We made music."

The close embrace style of Tango was created for small spaces: Intimate, romantic, and passionate. Marta's living room was perfect. Her foyer had the same floor surface, which, when needed, became part of the dance area.

I felt the quiet around me as we danced. We had an audience. Even Marta came into the living room to watch.

I have said it many times, "Sex is gratifying in many ways. Tango is more so."

Today, I knew that I would dance with all the women in Marta's living room. I would be their taxi dancer.

I had completely forgotten about Matin and Javier. When I sat down, they were both on the patio. I sensed they were finished dancing for today. Their effort to diminish the "gringo" from Nueva York did not go as planned.

Nor would it ever. Certainly not today.

The Grammar Lesson

In my sixth year of dancing the Argentine tango and having traveled to Buenos Aires more than a dozen times, I realized that it would be a help to my dancing if I learned to speak Spanish.

The thought of learning Spanish brought back uncomfortable memories. I recognized it could expose my inadequacies of English grammar. The improper use of the English language was my inheritance for growing up in Brooklyn during the 1960s. It didn't help that, throughout my academic years, I studied the science of symbols and numbers. So it was with a modest degree of trepidation that I enrolled with Arda, my wife, in a beginners' course in New York City. We survived the introductory course and moved onto the next level. Going to class once or twice a week was not a death-defying experience. It was almost pleasant. We agreed that our upcoming trip to Argentina should include a two-week immersion course in learning Spanish.

I found a school in Cordoba which was the old capital of Argentina when it was under the colonial rule of Spain. Cordoba is famous for its 17th and early 18th century European architecture. Besides, the Spanish spoken there was the Spanish you would hear if you went to Spain. Here, we would be on the ground floor of properly learning the language as it was intended. Additionally, choosing Cordoba gave us the opportunity to study in the daytime and dance in the evening.

I was nervous. The course would be challenging. I have had difficulties in the past controlling my competitiveness and insecurities when studying with Arda. I needed to have as many "learning Spanish" books that I could pack into my suitcase. I booked a suite at the Cordoba hotel. A suite would ensure we had enough space to spread our books out, comfortably.

My nightmare was now a reality. I was in a class with five others, all of whom were attending a university in Europe. Most were traveling through South America to expand their knowledge and understanding of Spanish culture.

The teacher, a woman in her late twenties, conducted the class in Spanish. She talked fast. At the end of the class day we were given, it seemed, another five hours of homework. The study/work table in the classroom was a community table that could hold up to eight students comfortably. It was round. It made it very difficult to be uniquely distant from the teacher. I named it "the students of the round table."

Every day, my goal was to survive the day and then another, until I completed the course. Learning was a tool in my survival kit. I did not realize that it was my only tool. The teacher used the blackboard to teach, and still, she was close enough to me that I could smell her perfume. There was no place to hide. Looking at the papers in front of me and not wanting to look at the teacher or anybody else for that matter did not work well in a five-hour class with five other students. I was in trouble. I started this journey with a knowledge deficit of English grammar. Now, I had to learn English grammar *while* learning Spanish grammar to succeed. There was no other way.

Thankfully, the suite at the Cordoba Hotel had two bedrooms, plus a living room and a small kitchen. I was able to lay out all the books on the floor, sit at the table_and select which book was needed to finish the homework assignment. We studied every day from 3 p.m. to 9 p.m. We studied vocabulary, verb conjugations, the use of pronouns, and the ever-present requirement to master the outliers of Spanish grammar.

Those elements of the language that created their rules all engendered the same fear in me that I experienced when I was in the third and fourth grade of my childhood parochial school. That feeling of not being able to understand what they were trying to teach me, being unable to absorb the material, and the most damaging: developing poor study habits. I was in constant fear in the classroom, then and now. Different times, different reasons, same fear. I thought *everyone would see how unprepared I am, and how little I have learned.*

Time, I needed more time to study and could not remember what I just studied. So I would study it again, but the state of being unprepared never left me. After 9 p.m., strange as it seemed, we went out to eat and dance.

I remember one evening, it was no later than seven, when Arda jumped up threw her books on the floor and said, "Let's go eat and dance early tonight."

I looked up at her and saw this grand smile, and I, too, threw my books on the floor and shouted "*vamanos.*" We had as they say "a very good night."

I tried to appear calm amongst my classmates, maybe asking a question or two, but all the time waiting for the end. Can I do the two weeks without imploding? How many times would the teacher accept "I don't know" from me? During my afternoon study periods at the hotel, I am sure I drove Arda mad with my questions. The questions were always the same, always looking for the edge that would help "the brain work." Without realizing that I was, in fact, learning the language, I continued to exist in my semi-paranoid state.

During the second week of the course, I raised my hand in class and asked a question in Spanish. The teacher stopped and looked at me as if she had never seen me in her class. She smiled and said: *"Es Una Buena Pregunta."* All of a sudden, all five students directed their attention to me as if I just answered the riddle of which came first, the chicken or the egg. Many *"muy biens"* were whispered to me by my classmates.

That evening we, again, went out to our favorite tango restaurant and danced the night away. The restaurant played traditional tango music which I prefer over the more modern music. Unlike learning Spanish, I knew how to dance the tango. On the second Friday of our two-week stay, Arda and I were invited to dance on stage at the restaurant. We were chosen both for our dancing ability and because we were visitors from *Nueva York*. These nights of dining and dancing helped me feel more at ease in using what I learned in the classroom.

The following night was the night before the final examination. It would determine whether I moved to the next level or had to repeat the past two weeks. I decided to stay up all night and study. I had never studied with such conscientiousness before—not in high school, college, or graduate school. For me, this was serious stuff. Now I had a chance, a small chance, to get a passing grade. I studied hard, but would it be enough?

Argentina serves strong coffee, and that is what was needed the morning of my trial. We did not say much as we walked to school. All exams were given on this last day. The school and the classrooms were quiet and orderly. Fistfuls of sharpened pencils and notepads were all you saw on the desks. Was I ready? I don't know, but I was there to take the test, to prove to myself that hard work and tenacity paid off. The test lasted two hours. It had multiple-choice questions, comprehension, both oral and written—true-or-false questions on second-year grammar. It was a comprehensive exam. The time given was not enough for me; I used every minute.

The waiting began the moment I put my pencil down. I did not know if I passed. I, as usual, thought the worst. Since the instructor only had five test papers to grade, she announced that she would return the exam with our final grade in less than an hour, or just after our lunch which the whole class attended. I didn't think we would get the results back that day. I thought we would be long gone from

114

Cordoba before the exam results were given back.

The nightmare continued. Arda and I had to attend the lunch. These last two weeks concluded the immersion session for the school. There was a ceremony attached to ending the summer sessions. Not for me. I chose to hide in an empty classroom. I looked unusually somber, sitting at a desk studying my notes as if there were another test to come.

During the next few minutes or so, two students from my class saw me and told me that our teacher was looking for me. Arda was already at the lunch table enjoying the lunch meal. I decided to join her as my classroom sanctuary was no longer useful. She too had received her exam papers. Her grade was a seventy eight. That was low for Arda, but being that she had to contend with me, I could imagine that I cost her points.

All my life I had the awful habit of not "facing the music." I'd rather postpone the expected bad news. Here I was, unwilling to acknowledge the grade of my two-week immersion course as if my avoidance or acceptance would change the grade. Alone I sat at a desk in the empty classroom, too embarrassed to man up.

As expected, *La Profesora* found me. "*Hola*, Herve, there you are. I have been looking all over for you. I have your test results."

She smiled broadly and handed me the test papers. The papers were folded so I could not see the grade. I thanked her, and before I could open them, she said out loud: "*Buenisimo, senor.*"

I had the papers in my hand, and I slowly unfolded them. On the first page was a hand-written note congratulating me on my efforts in the classroom and my accomplishments over the last two weeks. Written in a flowing script was the number seventy-two.

I passed, with a seventy-two. I passed the course! I looked for Arda and finally found her talking in Spanish with our classmates. She saw the look on my face and smiled. I whispered very softly, "Seventy-two, a seventy-two." All the work, the angst, the self-doubt, the anxious moments, all vanished. I was almost giddy. We both laughed and had the most enjoyable afternoon of our trip.

I never did forget those weeks in Argentina and the life-changing experience that a seventy-two in a two-week Spanish course had on the rest of my life. It felt good to retire that suitcase of demons. Miraculously, I lost my Brooklyn accent.

The Lady with the Coach Bag

The weather report indicated that today was the last cool day before the temperature would spike into the 70s. Spring had finally arrived. I thought this would be a good day to bring Chelsea, my blue grey miniature Pincher to town, and show her off as I sat outside my favorite coffee shop, sipping my hot coffee before I switched to iced coffee.

Lisa, one of the morning baristas, who was familiar with my usual coffee order, noticed my arrival with Chelsea.

"That's a beautiful dog you have. What is the breed?" she asked. "I haven't seen that breed before and I thought I saw them all. My shift will be over in a few; I would like to take a closer look at your dog."

"Do you have a few minutes for a rather interesting story of how I came to have Chelsea?" I asked.

"Sure," she replied.

Lisa returned five minutes later and made herself comfortable sitting next to Chelsea.

"Simply put, I won Chelsea in a poker game in Las Vegas."

I paused to let that thought sink in, but I think Lisa felt it was longer than a pause. I could sense the anxiety of questions building up in her mind. It was best to keep the narrative of the trip focused on that eventful night.

I began, "Las Vegas had been seeing tough times the past few years. The housing crash had been devastating to the Las Vegas economy. That night, the casino I entered reflected those conditions. The poker tables were empty save for two tables that had barely enough people at each table to make a game interesting. There was plenty of room at either one, so it made no difference which table I chose to sit at and play. For so few people, the betting was pretty solid. All the players, it seemed, thought they had winning hands this evening. They were not conservative. In fact, I was the most conservative. I'm not complaining. I was winning.

As the dealers were changing shifts, a woman wearing a big hat and oversize sunglasses sat down at the table. Not an uncommon casino outfit. What stood out most about her was the coach handbag. It was the largest coach bag I had ever seen. As she put the bag down I noticed the bag move. Whatever moved in the bag was alive. It wasn't just a shift of goods to balance out the bag's contents. I wouldn't have given the lady in the hat with the big sunglasses much thought, but I was curious about the contents of the bag.

A pretty woman in her mid to late 40s, her dress matched her coach bag, as did her shoes. The cluster of rings on her fingers was impressive. The diamond ring was outstanding. With few players at the table, you can concentrate on the players and get to know their *style*. You can interpret *style* any way you want. For me, it gives certain clues to their betting tendencies. As it happens in poker, I and one other player at the table were on a hot streak, and one person was turning out to be the big loser. As I said, the people at the table were not conservative in their betting. I was up about four thousand, and the other player was up about six. My math said the lady with the coach bag was down more than ten big ones. The house was down a little. The other two players were about even.

The *Coach Lady,* inconspicuously, kept looking at her bag. It seemed that I was the only person that paid any attention to her and her bag.

As happens in card games when you have one or two big winners, you also have one or two big losers. These were the table conditions going into what seemed like the last hand for the lady and her fellow loser. In poker, more often than not, players always run out of chips. Translate that to "out of money." It didn't help that this was a *no limit* betting hand.

The "coach lady" exhibited all the signs of being forced out of the game. Moreover, as happens so very frequently in high stakes poker, the loser begins to look for other assets on their person to continue in the game. She took off her diamond ring and put it on the table for all of us to see. "It's worth at least ten thousand without the setting," she said. "I will take four thousand for it and if I lose I will buy it back tomorrow." Everyone at the table remained very quiet.

Without looking at her so she could not read my intentions, I said, "I have an alternate offer for you to consider."

All eyes were on me as I continued: "I will give you the four thousand for your coach bag with the contents that's in it. No changes, no comments, either you accept the offer or you do not. There will be no buybacks of the contents in your bag. If you lose the hand and cannot give me the four thousand back here and now, I take the bag and walk." Everybody at the table thought I was crazy. I thought so as well, thinking to myself, I bet it's a dog. If not, I will give it back to her. If I were right, I just bought my wife a wonderful birthday present. The Lady accepted my wager.

The dealer called the table back to play, and the lady lost the hand on the turn of the next open card. I took the rest of my chips off the table and asked her for the bag. Stone-faced, she handed the bag to me and without another word I got up from the table and went to my room.

I could hardly wait until I got in the room to open up the bag. But I did wait. Once inside I opened the bag and there looking back at me was this beautiful blue miniature Pincher, peering straight into my eyes. I thought it was smiling at me. I lifted her up and verified that she was a female. Her leash, dog food, and AKC registration tags were all in the bag. She appeared very happy to be in my company. I guess she liked men.

I made a bed for Chelsea and brought her a steak and potatoes dinner. I wanted her to be happy and content with the subtext of hoping she will sleep the night through, which she did. I had a little difficulty getting her out of the hotel for a morning walk. Thankfully, the hotel had a grass dog walking area. I walked Chelsea and cleaned up after her. I used the big coach bag to transport Chelsea back and forth to the hotel room.

Of course, as I expected, the lady with the big hat and sunglasses was waiting for me in the lobby. I brought Chelsea upstairs to the room and let her run around. I put a DO NOT DISTURB sign on the door and went down to talk with the lady with the oversized sunglasses.

She began, "There is eight thousand in the purse, please take it and give me back my dog." "Not happening," I began. "It is a night and morning too late. I did not win Chelsea to have her bought back at a higher price. This was a one-way transaction," I said. "You shouldn't have bet your dog. All it means is that your gambling needs exceed the love for your dog. That will not happen with me. Chelsea will be happy, and so will my wife. The lady with the big hat and oversize sunglasses never did take either off, nor did she say goodbye to me. She just stood up and left. I suspect she had used Chelsea in the past to cover her table wager when her money ran out. I didn't think I would see her again.

Lisa looked at me and then at Chelsea and smiled. "Have you been back to Vegas since?" She asked.

"No", I said, "and I have no intention of going back." I winked and said, "That would be as foolish as the lady in the big hat and large coach bag. Let's go Chelsea; it's time to visit others."

The Magic Mountain

The oncoming mother of all storms scared everybody off the mountain; in fact, it scared everybody for miles around. The weather channel described it as the once-in-a-hundred-years "nor'easter." The gas and electric company shut down all service to the mountain and the surrounding towns. No gas in the village to run the generator. The doomsayers were correct in their prediction. No matter, I'm not leaving. The winds came and didn't leave. They brought a blanket of Arctic air that covered the entire Appalachian Mountains.

Today, the second day without power, I woke up at 5 a.m. and began to load firewood into the fireplace. It was cold in the house, not freezing yet, but soon. I got the fire going and planted myself in front of it until I warmed up. A peanut butter sandwich and a cold glass of water were this morning's breakfast. I went back to bed until daylight. *Notes from the mountain, day two.*

I have run out of the water I put into the bathtub that was to be used to flush the toilet.

Now I have to go to a small pond near the property and fill up two five-gallon buckets. Still have bottled water to brush my teeth and wash my face. Have not shaved in a week. Soon nobody will recognize me. I could easily pass for a needy in NYC. I need my coffee.

Tired. Worked hard today. Cold. Going to bed. *Notes from the mountain, day four, I think.*

Thought it was cold the night before. Not so. Last night was the winner, below twenty degrees and trending lower. Tonight more of the same. The fire in the fire pit (which I use for cooking) was so intense I thought someone would see it and call the state police. The water outside froze, could not clean the coffee pot. It was cold. The smell of food and the fire had attracted all kinds of animals, both local and not so local. The yellow flames must have been visible for miles. Raccoons, who are usually afraid of fire, were the first to move into the circle around the pit. Probably one family. The deer were inching up to the circle and in the shadows cast by the fire, I saw what I thought were two gray coyotes.

I did not move much from my strategic spot next to the pit. My motionless posture gave the coyotes courage to move into the light of the fire. It was then that I realized they were not coyotes but beautiful gray wolves. Wolves and I have a long history together. They have always been my protector in times of need. Until now, I didn't think I was in any danger but their appearance made me think about my precarious living conditions. They were involved, as you will learn, with my safety before, always to let me know that all will be well. I would not be here without them.

So here they were again, to tell me that, if needed, help was near. The wolf closest to the fire was the alpha female; she was big and beautiful with glowing blue eyes. If you didn't know any better, you would think they were attracted exclusively to the warmth and smell of food from the fire pit. They both sat down and started to howl at the moon. Their eyes were now ruby red. They didn't appear to be interested in me; later that night when I decided to go into the house, that is after the rum was finished, I left some food for them. Who knows, maybe I truly have protection. In this weather, I slept like a dead man left alone in the bitter cold.

Saturday (last night) was the coldest day and night of the year, but I am beginning to think every new day and night is the coldest of the year. I'm losing track of time. The water I use for the toilets, coffee, and washing up was frozen. I'm now taking water from another pond, which is farther from the house. I still have enough wood to burn in the fireplace and the pit outside. Most of the daylight hours are spent finding felled trees and cutting them into sizes I could split. It takes four to five hours of my time each day. In yesterday's posting, thank you Wi-Fi, on the storm site I asked if anybody would like to keep me company. Just testing to see if there were any other crazy people out there.

Being alone is probably the most difficult for me. My only daytime companion is a tom turkey. He's a good listener, but a lousy talker. *Notes from the mountain, day (I don't know).*

Dunnia, a woman from New York, posted back. Said she "wanted to experience a night without any power or household amenities," but she was mostly excited about meeting the wolves I described in my previous post. It was quite unexpected, but exciting. I needed the company. I again tried to shave, but that was impossible. I would tear my face with a cold razor and no shaving cream. What was I even thinking? It is a task just to survive. I posted back to Dunnia to find out if she was familiar with the Metro North train line, which had recently restored partial service going up the Hudson. Fortunately, I still had a little gas in the truck to pick her up. We agreed that she would get up here before dark. The station was empty. People were not coming back to a place without power, heat, and fresh food.

The 5:05 train pulled into the station and three people got off. Although completely covered from head to toe with a fake fur winter coat, I could tell it was Dunnia. She was unmistakable. The other two commuters were undeniably men dressed for the arctic.

The winter coat covered the haji she wore. It took more than a moment to realize that she was an exotic beauty from a faraway land. Between the cold, and the shock of meeting her, I found it hard to speak. And I certainly didn't know what to say. "What brings you up to these parts of New York?" I mumbled.

Dunnia was more composed. "I read your blog about the wolves visiting your campfire and it intrigued me."

"Why the wolves?" I asked.

"Your post triggered my memory of growing up in the Atlas Mountains in Tunisia. The mountains were and are famous for their free ranging wolf population. The wolf packs are always led by an alpha female. Every summer I worked at the base of the mountain protecting my family's sheep. One summer I was befriended by an alpha wolf, who kept me company and protected me for many years from other wolves and thieves who came to steal my sheep. Your description of the alpha female brought back very strong memories. Especially your comment about the wolf's eyes changing color. Very few people know this about alpha wolves."

Again, I loaded up the fireplace and the pit, hoping that we would have heat, both inside and outside the house, to keep us warm wherever we were. It was still bitterly cold, day and night. Food keeps without spoiling at these temperatures, and I still had lots of chicken and sweet potatoes to put on the grill. To go along with my gourmet meal, I opened a bottle of my favorite rum from Guatemala. This would guarantee inner warmth. It was smooth, toasty, and put a rosy hue on our faces. We were on course to finish this bottle of firewater well before the full moon appeared overhead. I knew Dunnia's behavior was inconsistent with traditional Muslim customs. We were here for reasons that only the mountain and the wolves knew.

"What brought the wolves to you? They seem to be very comfortable around you," she asked.

"I know why they are comfortable around me; I grew up with them, but I have no idea why they would be so friendly to you."

The rum made me feel warm, nostalgic, romantic and philosophical, all at the same time. I was a little tipsy and had the feeling I was an actor on stage with Dunnia, and a cast of eager listeners comfortably seated around the pit were waiting for me to relive the story of how the *wolves* saved my life.

"Ten years ago, I felt my life was going nowhere, and I decided to visit a Shaman whom I had read about in a news article. Trained in Peru, she worked with the Hopi Indians in the red mountains of Arizona and New Mexico. In our first meeting she asked me to imagine the following while meditating:

> You are in an underground tunnel which is without light but not completely dark. On both sides of the tunnel is a ledge running its entire length. The ledge acts as a showcase for all the earth and sky animals that inhabit our planet. You will recognize many of the animals that you pass. Look at each one, but keep moving. The animal that looks back at you and follows your gaze is your earth animal, your guide, your protector. Be assured, that animal will protect you in time of need.

"These were my instructions from the Shaman. I closed my eyes and went into a state of meditation. Soon, I pictured the underground tunnel, and I saw the animals standing on the ledges. The ledges were crowded with animals. All sizes and shapes. Was I running or walking? Not sure, but I was moving past what appeared to be a diorama of all the animals on earth. I was hoping one of them would stare back at me. What would happen if I didn't have an earth animal to protect me? Would I be safe, or not? Does everyone have a corresponding earth animal? These were my thoughts as I walked (or ran) through the tunnel.

"Out of nowhere, I felt a pair of eyes watching and following me. Turning to my right, there, on the ledge, was a silver gray wolf staring at me. I didn't know how many animals I had passed; I only knew the wolf satisfied my quest. In my mind I shouted, *The wolf is my earth animal.*

"I was sure at that moment that the silver wolf had heard me. The tunnel ended very soon after my recognition and acknowledgement of its presence."

The feeling around the fire pit was magical. It appeared the animals were indeed listening to me as I related my story to Dunnia. They kept their gaze fixed on both of us. I took another swig of rum and continued.

"As I continued on my personal journey to the magic mountains of northern Arizona, in the darkness of winter, on the longest night of the year and probably the coldest, I had climbed what I thought was a trail, well known and presumably not difficult. Reaching the top of the mountain, much to my surprise, I realized there were two paths going down. I had no idea which one would take me down. I had lost my way and was not prepared to spend the night where I was. It was cold and getting colder. Not more than twenty feet down the left side of the fork were two wolves waiting for me. I sensed they were there for no other reason but to guide me. As I walked toward them, they turned and began to walk down the trail. I knew they would lead me down the steep mountain pass with all its hidden footfalls. Most assuredly, without them, the night would have taken me away. The white fur of the alpha female, the bigger of the two, reflected the moonlight a good ten feet in all directions. Better than a flashlight. They were gone when I finished my descent down to the base of the mountain."

Not a soul moved while I told my story. It seems even the wind took a break from blowing to listen to my strange encounter in the mountains of Arizona.

Another swig of rum and I continued. "The second meeting came ten days later. The red mountains of Arizona, legend has it, are more magical after sundown and most magical an hour before sunrise. My last assignment from the Shaman was to greet the sunrise at the top of "The Great Spirit Mountain." I began my climb in total darkness an hour before sunrise. The path was steep and very rocky. My flashlight was completely inadequate for this assignment. It was difficult to hold it and climb at the same time. The last section was too steep for me to continue going up, and I knew at this point in the climb that it would be too difficult to get down. I was stuck. I could neither go up nor down. Frozen in time I just stared into the night.

"It was not more than a moment later before I felt the existence of another being close by. I turned and looked up to see a man with a full head of silver hair and laser-like blue eyes standing at the top of the pitch looking back at me. When he saw I had acknowledged his presence, he turned and continued the climb to the top of the mountain. We did not speak. I followed the radiance of his silver hair to the top, over, and down the other side until I was safely off the mountain. He, like the wolves before him, disappeared into the sunrise. I had no doubt who he was. Since then I have had no other experience with my protectors; until now."

I looked at Dunnia and noticed the alpha female was sleeping on her lap. She looked back at me and I saw royal blue eyes where they once were brown. Stroking the wolf, she said, "We have a connection; what it is I don't know," she whispered, not to disturb the wolf.

The fire needed more wood, and I needed more firewater. I had to get away from the fire to clear my head and cool off. Going to the house to get my last bottle of rum would be well worth the effort. Standing up was not easy. *Easy boy, you can do it,* I thought to myself.

"We need more wood and rum!" I shouted to no one in particular, wanting to make sure she heard me.

Dunnia knew the two wolves that warmed themselves around the fire pit were the same two wolves that saved me ten years ago, and I knew when I saw the color change in Dunnia's eyes that she was the silver haired man, who too saved me ten years ago.

Who would believe me? Two wolves: a variety of nocturnal animals, a shape shifter from the Middle East, and me, gazing up at the stars and listening to the wood crackle, keeping warm around the fire on Magic Mountain in the middle of an extreme winter storm.

I smiled and thought: *I'm losing my grip on reality and love it.*

Notes from the mountain.

The Wheelchair

I made reservations for my Florida vacation on December 21, the day of the winter solstice. Florida was my escape. Ten days in the sun was all I needed to keep me balanced and get me through the remaining winter months.

Two weeks before my scheduled departure date, on another sub-zero morning, I tried to get out of bed and realized I couldn't stand. The pain was sharp and hot. The slightest pressure on either foot made me jump in agony. I felt the whip lashes across the soles of my feet with every step. First, my left foot, "thwack," then my right foot, "thwack." The pain was shooting straight up my leg. It only stopped when I crawled on my knees and remained off my feet. The soles of my feet were beet red.

I held onto the wall and walked, or should I say hobbled on the sides of my feet. It took a while, but I was able to get to the bathroom. The sight of the thirteen steps down to the main level of the house brought the horror of my days in Vietnam front and center. How am I going to get down the stairs? I could just crawl back into bed, but then I would have to stay there. *Crawl and use the walls! That's how you got out of your foxhole. No one helped you then.*

Both ankles and soles of my feet were swollen. Is it possible to have swollen soles? I could see my ankles were swollen maybe my soles were just inflamed. Loose fitting cotton socks barely made it around my ankles and I knew that I would not be able to fit into any shoes or boots in my closet. My crocks, which I rarely wore, were the only footwear wide enough for my feet.

By the end of the first week, I had taken a number of blood tests for all types of arthritis, diabetes, osteoporosis, old age, and lastly Lyme disease. The results came back a few days later with a positive read for Lyme disease. I was shocked! Lyme disease in the middle of winter? It must have been in my system for quite some time, dormant until now.

By this time, I was grateful to have a condition with a name. Now I could begin treatment. High doses of antibiotics and Tylenol. A month's worth of antibiotics taken twice a day was the regimen. Initially, there was very little change in my condition. The soles of my feet were still painful. Getting from one room to another was exhausting. Any weight, however slight, hurt— even the soft touch of my down comforter. I finally understood what "painful to the touch" meant. You could not call how I got around *walking. Travel? How was that possible?*

* * *

The night before my scheduled departure, I decided to cancel my trip. The image of walking to the gate and standing in line to go through security sent chills up and down my spine. I knew I couldn't survive a middle-seat selection. I had images of not being able to stand or use the bathroom. This was a four-hour flight.

My wife was not going to let me stay home. She knew I would recuperate faster and be more comfortable not having to get around in the snow and freezing temperatures.

She convinced me that it would not be as bad as I imagined it would be. "Have them give you a wheelchair. In fact, you can reserve one, and before you know it, I'll be down there to help."

That wheelchair stuff would never happen, but I didn't have the energy to argue with her. Either way, I was going.

I had been a cross-country runner who ran with sprained ankles and limped through airports on crutches, but I never needed a wheelchair.

I pictured old people in wheel chairs being shuffled through security and into their seats aboard the airplane—always the first to be put on the plane, and the last to be taken off. I didn't mind the courtesies extended to the elderly or infirm, I just didn't want to be part of their routine. This meant staying out of a wheelchair. With my backpack filled to capacity, hanging off one shoulder, and my crocks as footwear, I approached the airline's check in area. The line attendant saw me hobbling toward him and, without ceremony, offered a chauffeured wheelchair to assist me to my gate.

I looked at him, thinking to myself, *I'm not a cripple or an old man. I've hurt worse than this,* and politely refused his gesture, patting him on the shoulder as I went by him to the ticketing agent to get my seat assignment. I was fourth in line.

The ticketing agent smiled as I approached and told her my tale of woe and why I absolutely needed an aisle seat. Before I could finish she inquired: "Shall I get you a wheelchair with an attendant to assist you to your gate?"

She had a beautiful smile, and I felt the good intention of her offer. Still, I wanted to pretend that I didn't need help. However, everyone else saw I needed help and in simple ways, people told me so. Being proud and a bit of a jerk, I said, "How did you know I needed a wheelchair?"

"I could see you needed help. Wait here! I will have the attendant bring you a wheelchair." She was busy and had little time for small talk. On another day, I might have lingered at the counter and told her how attractive she was. Hard to do when you are discussing wheelchairs.

"Is it a long walk to the gate?"

"Yes, it is," she replied.

I tried smiling and looked for a modest response in kind, but it was hard coming to terms with the realization that I needed help. How humbling! How embarrassing! Where were my sunglasses when I needed them?

I followed the agent's gaze to the rear of the ticketing line. She had made eye contact with an older woman and indicated she come down to the counter with a wheelchair. I was told to stand aside.

When the woman reached me, she whispered in my ear, "Solo, Solo?"

"Si, soy solo," I responded in my broken Spanish. Did she think I was deaf as well as infirm?

"Ok, you sit and hold," she said as she began to maneuver the wheel chair through the hustle and bustle of the ticketing area.

Moving at almost dangerous speed, she yelled out to me, "Give me your boarding pass and your license!"

I joked aloud that I was being robbed but nobody paid any attention to me. Certainly not Grandma. Even though, given the present conditions, she was certainly more physically fit than the person she was pushing around in *her* chair.

I was too embarrassed to look up during my trip through security for fear of being viewed as *just another old man joining other old men being wheeled through security.* Best to just keep my head down and let my driver do the dirty work. I didn't want the world to see me like this. Being in a wheel chair, physically unfit, brought to mind the mantra I have kept of myself for the better part of my life. *Don't let them see you hurtin'.*

"Excuse me, excuse me" the woman said as people in front of us jumped aside.

I tried to tell her to stop. I wanted to go to el bano, but she didn't hear me or didn't care. I wanted to buy a sandwich for the trip and that request too, was ignored. We went down a number of ramps that were barely wide enough to take the wheelchair. Then through another side door and another and behold we were at the departing gate.

My physically fit driver, Grandma, handed me over to an attractive gate attendant, who asked if I wanted to be wheeled onto the plane. It was well before any boarding announcements were made.

"It is easier to wheel you into an empty plane now, before we begin to board," she informed me.

"No thank you, I'll walk onto the plane when my zone is called. For now, I would just like to sit in the waiting area."

All this time my driver was filling out papers for the gate attendant which I understood meant that she was finished, and the gate attendant was now responsible for my person. I put a bill into her hand and thanked her. "Gracias."

I was promptly wheeled to a convenient part of the waiting area. I took a seat close to the food shops and the men's bathroom. My wheelchair was placed in an area with a dozen others; waiting for the next group of needy travelers. I was happy to be rid of my four-wheeled transport.

Seated, I took a moment to catch my breath and to realize how much I had needed the attention and the unsolicited assistance and courtesies that I had received from the airline attendants. I never would have made it through the lines. Their help was entirely unexpected and very much appreciated. I couldn't have done it any other way. I had to admit to myself that I was vulnerable and needed help. This brief visit to the world of my future scared the hell out of me!

There might be a ray of sunshine in all of this if I can get beyond my own self-delusions. There was help when I needed it, and now I know there will be help in the future should I need it.

Maybe this was a winter's Fairy tale? The next day, I paraphrased a famous song "I'm Walking in Sunshine."

Barely.

Mind Games

Christmas Eve – The First Night

"Give me water; the ice cubes you gave me to suck on are all gone."

"Hey, Man. You can't have any water after your operation," said the orderly, an imposing Jamaican man. "Doctor's instructions. You just come out of surgery and water will interfere with the medication they put in you. Man, you got to wait until the mornin' time."

"I'm so thirsty, I can barely open my mouth, Please, a little water."

I tried to get up, but he held me down. He looked big, really big. I was too weak to sit up.

"No, you can't do that; you'll hurt yourself."

He called for help through the intercom. Another male orderly came rushing into the room and saw me struggling to get out of bed.

"Dremand, hold his feet down, he's too strong for me!"

"Ok, I'll strap the belt around his feet and tie it to the railing. You do his arms."

I screamed for help, but that may have been my imagination. I do remember, for sure, using my legs to bend both railings into a pretzel. I tried to break the bed in two. I could not use my arms because the doctors had cracked open my chest, taken my heart out and put it into a pail while they replaced five of the arteries leading to my heart. Then they'd reset the heart and sewed the two halves of my chest back together. But that had been six hours ago.

I lost the battle against these two men. Exhausted, I passed out into a night of nightmares and restless dreams.

* * *

In the early winter of 2000 I decided to enter my first "50 and Over" road race. I had been riding recreationally for a few years and that winter I decided to see how good or bad I was as compared to others in my age category.

I was in the best shape of my life at that time. My blood numbers were excellent. My resting heart rate was low, and I could reach a maximum heart rate fifteen points above my age bracket. I could not remember the last time I'd had a cold. The winter training schedule had been rigorous: swimming and cross-country skiing in the early months, weight lifting during the later months, and always riding outdoors whenever the weather allowed. That was my routine for the next two years. I had, it seemed, an unlimited amount of energy and rosy cheeks. I felt healthy! There were days on the bike when I thought I was invincible.

Lying here, in the early morning, after a successful seven-hour heart operation and trying not to pay attention to the pain in my chest, I had time to review what my body had told me was wrong with *it,* and how I had paid no attention to its signals.

It was in the spring of 2003 that I had started to experience chest pains. No big deal, I was drinking a lot of black coffee and assumed it was heartburn. I started to take antacids.

Having used a heart rate monitor for training, I noticed the "heartburn" began to bother me at 128 beats per minute. At that rate, I was not working hard. The pain would increase if I tried to go faster and would decrease if I went slower. The following months, I found myself making all sorts of excuses to my bike buddies about why I had to slow down or even stop and get off my bike. My heart was working harder at much slower speeds. It was time for a checkup.

The winter was coming and the biking season would be over. It would be the perfect time to arrange a stress test. I made my appointment for the day after Thanksgiving, two weeks before my 64th birthday.

My wife, Arda, and I had tickets for a dance recital in New York the Monday before Thanksgiving. We arranged to meet at the theatre at 8 p.m. I was late and couldn't find parking nearby; the nearest parking lot was six city blocks away. Rather than walk, I ran to the theatre. Three blocks from the theatre, I developed severe chest pains and had to stop. I sat down on the curb, my feet resting in the street. People stopped and asked if I was okay and I said, "Yes—I just need to catch my breath." I sat there for the next five minutes. Slowly, I stood up and walked to the theatre. I said nothing to Arda about the incident. But I was in trouble and knew it.

Thanksgiving day it snowed most of the day. Unusual, but it happens. I thought about cancelling the following morning's appointment, and only at the last minute decided to go.

Friday, black Friday, felt that way: Cold, no sun, more snow on the roads than expected—I was glad I had my Saab to get me to the hospital. Unbeknownst to me, while driving, the hospital called my home to cancel the appointment. Of the three nurses scheduled to work that day, only one had shown up, and she wanted to go back home, fearful of the continuing snow accumulation. Learning that they could not get in touch with me, she felt obliged to stay and administer the test.

The parking lot was empty. An empty parking lot at a major hospital? Where were the emergency vehicles? I parked in front of the entrance and followed the lights leading me to the front desk.

"You must be Harvey," the receptionist said. "I'm happy to see you; your nurse was worried she had made the trip in for nothing. Everyone else cancelled for today."

She escorted me into the changing room and said, "She is waiting for you in the examination room."

I changed and went into the room.

"Don't rush; the doctor won't be here for another half hour. I'll take all of your vitals and prepare you for the stress test. He'll monitor the test. The doctor came in just as the nurse finished wiring me to the EKG machine.

"Good morning. Glad to see there are other crazy people out here besides me," he said, without looking at anyone in particular. Not waiting for an answer, he asked me, "Do you know what we're looking to measure?"

"Yes, I do."

"Okay. Before we begin, tell me what's going on with you?"

"I have chest pains when I exercise, and the pain is such that I can't continue to increase my aerobic activity beyond 128 bpm. It's too painful. The pain subsides if I reduce the activity level."

"Okay, let's get started; I'll come back in when the nurse has increased the difficulty to 128."

I'm sure he went into the next room to get a cup of black coffee. He returned just when my chest pains began and the heart monitor was approaching 128.

He looked at the EKG and stopped the test. "Put him on the table for an echocardiogram. Now!"

The rest of the examination showed severe blockage in two arteries.

"We'll schedule an angiocardiogram to find out without doubt how many arteries are affected. I'll schedule the exam for next week."

Looking straight into my eyes, he said, "Don't do any strenuous exercise over the weekend. In fact, don't do any exercise." Then he was gone. The receptionist gave me my appointment slip, and I left.

The results of the angiogram were not good. It confirmed almost one hundred percent blockages in two major arteries leading into the heart muscle with blockage of fifty percent in two others. My good health and rigorous training had allowed the blood to go into the heart muscle by creating a bypass artery and feed blood to the heart. But it had done little to alter the genetic structure I'd inherited from my parents, and its inevitable results.

The hospital cardiologist recommended immediate open-heart surgery. By "immediate" he meant: the day before Christmas. Obviously, not a good time to schedule such a serious operation. Everyone laughed it off.

* * *

Day Two

They were unstrapping me, and at the same time screaming at each other. The head nurse, the first in on the day shift, wanted to know who'd given the orders for the overnight *strap down*.

"You could've given him a heart attack and god knows what else. Call the neurology floor downstairs. I want to talk with the doctor on duty. Get a new bed in here and take out this mangled piece of crap. Get rid of it. Now!"

Her phone rang a few minutes later. All I could make out was, "Yes. Yes, and okay."

Turning to the orderlies, she said, "Prepare the patient for travel in his new bed. He's going downstairs to have a cat scan. The neurology floor wants to make sure he did not suffer any brain damage."

If it wasn't so bizarre I would have laughed out loud, but laughing with my chest so recently reconnected hurt too much. The head nurse turned to me and said, "Your son is coming in at nine to accompany you down to neurology."

Upon reflection, I realized *I've got to get out of this place. If last night is an example of hospital care, I'll be dead in a week. I have to figure out what I have to do to convince them I'm healthy enough to leave. What tests do I have to pass...?*

At nine, my son, Eli, helped wheel the bed into the hall and onto the elevator. As we got on, two orderlies were getting off... the same two orderlies that had strapped me down. They were arguing over which one was at fault the night before and neither seemed to notice who was in the bed.

I shouted, "Hey man, you got any water?" They heard me and turned as the doors shut.

"Dad, cut the shit."

We both laughed. Laughing is not good for me.

Of course, the brain scan showed no irregularities. I don't remember anything more because I passed out on the table. Eli, I suspect, helped wheel me back to the room. I was still asleep. I slept most of the afternoon.

Miraculously, the night was uneventful.

* * *

Day Three

The staff, at my request, moved a padded armchair into my room. They assumed it was for sitting up while I watched television and when guests visited. Not so! I slept in the chair. I slept in the bed during the day, but at night, I slept in the chair. I was taking no chances of a repeat performance by the staff. One night of insanity was enough.

I befriended the floor nurse, Flores, who seemed to be sympathetic because of what had happened on that first night. It was her nursing staff that bore the responsibility for the strap down.

Nurse Flores was not good for my heart, but great for my mind: A pretty woman who dressed well, she had a warm smile and soft hands. I enjoyed it when she took my blood. She had a way of caressing my fingers that created a tingle all the way up my arm and into my shoulder. I knew all my body parts were working, and my operation was a success.

Sitting in my newly-anointed throne, the padded chair, I asked Nurse Flores what physical and mental condition I had to be in before they released me.

"We don't use the word 'condition' in our evaluation," she said. "You have to know who you are: by stating your name, age, family connections, and having a certain grasp of current events. The neurologist will ask you a series of questions dealing with these subjects."

"I'd like to make an appointment with the neurologist. I want to be tested. Can we do that today?"

She looked at me and smiled. "I'll see what I can do."

"No, don't go yet. You mentioned something about the status of my physical condition; whom do I see about that?"

"Dr. Stairs. I can arrange that for you as well. He's a tough one."

The patient lounge gets the papers delivered every morning, along with a few weekly magazines. I was able to get there by myself with the aid of a walker. Between family visits and one or two walks to the lounge I was soon tired and longed for sleep in my padded throne. I remained most vigilant during the night hours. I slept in two-hour intervals, making sure I faced the entrance to my room and kept the night light on all night. I was a prisoner planning his escape. The third night passed without incident.

* * *

Day Four

Every morning, after walking to the lounge, I took *The Times* with me and returned to my room. Nurse Flores was in the room checking the furniture, or so it seemed.

"Surprise! I made an appointment for you with Dr. Stairs for this afternoon at four. I hope you are prepared. I suggest you take a nap before your appointment. Also, look sturdy on your walker. He notices these things."

Smiling, she said, "He enjoys using his name," and walked out.

A riddle; I am in the hospital with a cracked chest and I have a riddle to solve? *He enjoys using his name.* Stairs? Stairs? No, he wouldn't have me walk up flights of stairs. Moreover, if I walk up I must walk down. I wasn't sure I could do either.

I napped sitting on my throne and was not entirely surprised when Dr. Stairs walked into my room. The name on his ID tag spelled "Steers."

"Hi. Harvey?"

"Yes... Dr. Stairs?"

"Yes. Give me a moment to review your chart. I'm particularly interested in your first night here. I understand you pretzeled the bed?"

"Yes, they call me the pretzel maker on the floor."

The doctor smiled, and as he did, his glasses fell onto the bridge of his nose. He looked funny.

"Very interesting. Well then, we don't have to test for strength, just coordination and stamina. Follow me with your walker."

He began walking out of my room, then turned in the direction of the emergency exit. I was close behind. He pushed the door open, and we both walked onto the landing.

"Okay, Harvey, put your walker aside and grasp the handrail going up the stairs. Use your right hand to hold onto the rail. Go to the next landing—14 steps—and come back down the stairs using your left hand to hold onto the railing. Your heart is on that side. Take your time, but don't stop walking."

"Why the left hand on the heart side?"

He laughed, "Just to confuse you. That's why they call me Dr. Stairs, instead of Dr. Steers."

Walking down was harder than walking up. I was dizzy after my first two steps. I wanted to close my eyes, but I knew he was watching. My knees were beginning to shake, and I stopped smiling.

I said to myself: *You can do this; just concentrate on one step at a time.* I knew I was off balance. Something about the left side, what it was I didn't know. I was sweating by the time I finished. *If he asks me to take another step up or down, I'll faint.* But he didn't.

"Very good, Harvey. You passed two tests today. The stamina stair test, my favorite, and your comments about the heart being on the left side showed me that your cognitive functions are good. Congratulations! I'll tell Nurse Flores to notify the neurologist of today's results. Although, she may have additional questions to ask you."

He held the door open for me and my walker. Carefully and slowly, I walked to my room and collapsed in my chair. Visitors came and visitors departed. I didn't remember their coming or going. I simply wanted to sleep. Day Five would be the beginning of a new life for me.

* * *

Day Five

"You did it. Wake up, Mr. Harvey; you have a lot of work to do today if you are to be released tomorrow," Nurse Flores said while straightening my pillow.

"Tomorrow?" I said, rubbing my eyes. "What happened to now? Today?"

"Not possible. You are to be examined by your doctor and the staff neurologist. All forms must be handed in to the billing department before 3 p.m. Your doctor will not be here until early afternoon. So, another night and early exit tomorrow at 9 a.m. It's good for you to rest another day here. Your stitches will be cleaned later this afternoon and the pharmacy will deliver your medicines today."

Another night—in this crazy place! I wanted out today! However, I knew I'd better not give them a reason to keep me here any longer. Behave, Harvey. You can use the rest after yesterday's ordeal on the stairs. I'm a short timer; I knew I'd feel better after the doctor signed my release.

The neurologist walked into my room a little before noon. I was busy filling out papers for the admissions and discharge office.

"Good Morning, Mr. Hunt. I am Dr. Silva from neurology, and if you feel up to it, I have a few questions to ask you."

"Great, I've been expecting you."

She smiled and took her notepad out.

"Do you know what month it is? And possibly the day?"

"Yes, we are in December and today is Thursday."

"And how would you know that?

"I read *The Times* every day."

"Who is the current president? And, who was the president before him? And the president before him? Take your time."

I answered, "Busch, Clinton, Clinton." She smiled, noting my responses in her notebook.

I was tired. My head was beginning to hurt. I had to concentrate on the answers. I felt there was no room for error. She held the keys to my freedom.

"Can you tell me of any major current event that took place either locally or nationally during the past two months? Take your time."

In my mind, I reviewed all of the headlines I could remember reading in the Times. I did not look at her. It seemed as if time stood still.

"They caught Saddam Hussein in a cave," I blurted out, surprised at my answer.

Still smiling, she made more notes in her note pad. Nurse Flores and I said nothing. Turning to Nurse Flores, she said, "good to go" turned and left the room.

That afternoon, the room nurse washed and changed my bandages. My surgeon examined me and signed the release papers.

The fifth night passed without any drama.

* * *

Day Six

The sun was shining. A winter's sun. An abundance of morning light with little warmth. Nurse Flores volunteered to wheel me down to the first floor lobby. She also helped dress me. Arda and our eldest daughter were on their way to pick me up.

During my incarceration, I had been totally consumed with planning my escape. My pain, split chest, and lack of sleep had received little attention from me. I rarely needed additional medication or assistance.

The need to survive the institution had superseded little things like stitches popping and bouts of nausea from the medicines I was given. I thought often of being strapped down and what results that would have on my psyche. I knew I would never forget this week. I was glad to go home. Home!

I could not walk by myself for many days. Someone had to support me and monitor my rehabilitation. In time, months, I recuperated and was able to enjoy my activities without support or guidance.

157

That I did what I did on day one—survived the open-heart surgery, then the medieval straightjacket madness, and on days four and five, a Doctor's strange series of tests on the stairs of the hospital—this showed me how forceful and instinctual the will to survive can be.

Fear was the best medicine they gave me.

The Wood Stove

Simple, a wood stove sitting on a hearth in the corner of the living room. An innocent looking appliance. I feel strange calling my stove an appliance. Alternatively, maybe I am too sensitive. It is good looking, well designed, with a black exterior, and no legs to stand on. It has a sixteen by twenty-inch window, which allows me to see into its belly.

My stove eats pieces of wood and spits out of its stomach a fire so hot that ordinary metal would buckle and melt after three hours of intense heat. When harnessed this agent of fire becomes a wonderful source of heat. The heat warms the house in an evenness that neither gas nor electric can do, and neither can they soothe you, as you slowly close your eyes and dream of faraway beaches.

It may interest you to know that the true hero of this story, which may not be obvious, because of its transformation, is the log of wood that I feed into the stove's belly. It is this journey of the log that is so interesting and unnoticed. I can see the thoughts ticker tape across your forehead. "What journey? What journey is he talking about?"

Softly, in keeping with the ambience of the evening I invite the remaining guests, to gather around the red-hot stove as I tell the life story of a log.

"The other trees were bigger and fuller than it was, and eventually they took away the sunlight and drank the water in the ground that was intended for his roots. In time, the tree died. This life and death process occurred no more than four hundred yards from my living room window.

"The logs I am putting into the fire came from a tall tree that died a year before. The tree, once a lively, beautiful oak did not live long enough to see its best days. I felt, in a way that the tree had donated its life to me. All I had to do was cut the tree down, slice it into smaller pieces, split the rounds into beautiful logs, size them appropriately for our stove, and I'd know I would have heat for the winter.

Each log has, in it, an aroma that once was the scent of the mighty oak. As the log dries, and the wind blows over the log to remove its moisture, you can put your nose right next to the log and smell the oaky fragrance. It fills the air as it passes you by. Yes, it takes a good nose to smell the bouquet, but it is there.

"They say wood warms you twice. Once when you cut it and again when you burn it.

This is true. I have handled each log I put into the fire more than a few times. The log is known to me, it is personal. I was the midwife to this log. I changed it from a dead useless part of the tree to an object that gives warmth and contentment.

"I know what the fire dragon wants. It wants wood that is dry, aged, and dense. If I feed him what he wants, he gives me a clean, smokeless, efficient source of heat.

I have mixed feelings about my fire dragon. It has its mission, and an exalted mission it is. His purpose is, according to history, a purpose of the gods. I always have a tinge of sadness when I look into the widow and watch one of my logs disappear. One would think the log had done enough. But it continues to give even as it is turned to ash. I save its remains and mix it into my soil to help grow another tree.

"On those days of feeding the fire, I take the time to pour a glass of wine and toast to the past and future life of the tree for giving me this moment of tranquility on another cold and bleak winter's day."

I sensed they wanted to see me put a fresh log into the firebox; to behold, for themselves, with new insight, the hidden treasures of a log.

The Power of the Juice

A year had passed since that serendipitous week in January. I remember, because it was a surprisingly mild winter day, and I had decided to walk through Nordstrom's and check out the new styles in men's fashion. Hopefully, I could shop without having women intrude themselves into my shopping decisions. I sensed somebody watching me and turned just in time to avoid two beautiful black women crashing into me.

"Easy now," I said. "There are safer ways to meet than tackling me in the Men's Department."

Laughing, they apologized and said they urgently wanted to talk with me before I exited the store. I was flattered and introduced myself. "Hi, I'm Richard."

"We know who you are," said the more professionally dressed woman. "I am Lilliana and this is my Queen. Before we begin to tell you why we want to talk with you, we are curious why you are hiding in the Men's Department?" We could see you hiding behind the male mannequins. I needed to think before I opened up my mouth. "You won't believe this, but I created this pheromone by accident; it makes black women maybe all women want to be next to me, and touch me, as long as they are able to smell the fragrance of my cologne. I'm here, because I didn't think there would be a lot of women in the men's department. I was hiding."

Laughing, Lilliana said, "We know about your mixture. We call it the *juice, or the Pokako juice.* Haven't you observed certain body changes in the last month? The Queen was also able to grow your penis and darken your skin, or hadn't you noticed?"

"I did recognize the changes and thought I was losing my mind."

They both laughed and for the first time the Queen spoke. "You have a year to have fun, all the fun you can handle; Lilliana will supply you with the juice and you just go out get more of one particular ingredient that is vital in making the juice."

The queen finished her remarks by stating, "It will take a year of testing to come up with the right compound that is needed.

"Good luck Richard, enjoy the next year."

I did enjoy the next year. It was exciting even a little dangerous. The Pokako juice was a wonderful pheromone. I bedded many beautiful, interesting women. Besides their beauty and

African lineage, they were able to supply me with the squirt liquid I needed. I collected enough liquid to make Lilliana very happy.

The danger came from irate boyfriends, brothers, fathers and pimps. My newly-found penis length and darkened skin were perfect assets for my new occupation.

* * *

Time flies when you're having fun. It was a new year, but as usual, a cold winter in New York. The Queen had arranged a dinner party at Lilliana's apartment and asked us to join her. We were so to speak the board of listeners, Lilliana, Dr. Staci and I. Having finished a simple dinner of goat meat and rice, the Queen asked us to gather round her near the fireplace.

We formed a semicircle with the Queen at one end. As long as I had known the Queen I rarely saw her smile; it was the same tonight. Sitting upright in a high-backed chair that looked rather uncomfortable, she tried to smile, but was only partially successful.

"I am glad to see my friends around me," she said, "I have news for all. I know you have been wondering where we go from here with the Pokako juice.

"First, I would like to thank you for your efforts over the past year. I knew when we began this journey that the Pokako juice would have a better purpose than its current use as a phero-mone for humans.

"The use of the juice as an aphrodisiac was a fortuitous byproduct of the juice's true character and purpose. Its primary purpose was, as we found out, to expand a person's cognitive performance. But, as always, nature has funny ways to get us to the Promised Land.

"I understood that giving the juice to Richard in its natural state would increase the size of his penis and make his skin darker. This change allowed Richard to satisfy all the women he bedded. A satisfied woman squirts more liquid. By making Richard (as she nodded in my direction) more attractive to them, he insured their orgasm and subsequently their ejaculation of the vital liquid that we needed to make the juice. This liquid, as we know, is a principal ingredient in the Pokako juice. The second ingredient was the semen from any male of African descent.

"The combination worked, and we were able to test our theory of the juice's true purpose, which we did. Moreover, the production of the juice will take place in a state-of-the-art laboratory.

During the last year, a single thought had preoccupied us all. How did the Queen intend to fulfill the prophesy that her progeny would be the future leaders of the new world? Now, a year later, here we were, sitting around the fireplace, waiting to hear the Queen's grand design.

Looking down, the Queen pulled a few handwritten pieces of paper from her pocket. She studied them for a moment and began.

"The juice, when given in the appropriate dose to newly born African babies or to pregnant women of African descent, has the unique cell structure to absorb the juice into their bloodstream. We can verify that as the juice passes through the cell membranes in the babies' bodies, it is most readily absorbed by the cells in the brain. It nurtures the brain cells, and effects an extraordinary change in its chemistry." Recognizing she had our complete attention, she continued.

"Early tests have shown a dramatic increase in brain cell count as well as an increase in brain size. Additionally, at that early age the volume of blood traveling to the brain with the help of the juice is dramatically increased. The increase of blood flow to the brain is extremely beneficial. Think of it as blood doping. More oxygenated blood brings more oxygen to vital parts of the brain...

"The brain, as we know, has two distinct physical sides that represent two distinct areas of brain function. When babies of African descent are given the Pokako juice a paradigm shift takes place. The child will now be able to access both sides of the brain simultaneously.

"To accomplish this feat, the power of the brain would have to increase substantially. The juice does increase the physical size of the brain and by default the number of brain cells. The child, and later as an adult, will have the attributes to solve complex problems in half the time. Enough additional brain power to compete with today's powerful computers."

* * *

Silence, complete silence. We were all thinking "super person," but nobody said a word. I listened as my world of outstanding sex, with a penis that grows on command, with women of unparalleled beauty and unquenchable sex drives, disappears and morphs into areas of government, education, medicine and other worldly endeavors to improve the lives of mankind. I couldn't let the Queen read my mind and see how selfish I was. I felt my penis getting smaller, permanently.

She continued, "Dr. Marks and I understood the juice's power in generations to come, but what about now? What could the juice do for my people now? What immediate and tangible results could Dr. Marks show his Board of Governors, now?

"The doctor was interested in my year-long search to find a cure for sickle cell anemia He wanted to test synthetic Pokako juice in other areas of medicine as well. Now, they are making a few ounces of the juice a day. He wanted to bring that up to liters; to have more of his research team involved in the development to cure the genetically transmittable sickle cell anemia disease. To budget for the funds, he needed to know everything about the Pokako juice and for that matter, the historical background of the Queen as well."

Finally, a big smile appeared on her face. I guess she liked talking about herself in the third person.

Reviewing her notes, she continued. "I told him I would prepare a paper giving him the information he needed.

"Where it came from? The ingredients? The shelf life, etc. and when the juice was first introduced and used in Africa. I anticipated his request and was prepared, with help, to have the final report on his desk by next week.

"It was important, before I presented the story of the Pokako juice, that I had all the facts about my ancestors and the history of my tribe in some chronological order." Looking at the faces around her, she continued. "I shall read you what I wrote to Dr. Marks."

Many centuries ago, when my people inhabited the midsection of the African continent, the tribal elders had the responsibility of keeping us safe from marauding tribes living to the north of us.

When attacked, we could defend ourselves and eventually the fighting would stop and peace would return. Every mid-century, or so it seems, the regions peace would explode like a volcano, for no obvious reason. After we tired of fighting, and the smoke subsided, peace would rise from the smoldering ashes.

What we did not understand, nor did we know how to "fight" were airborne diseases: viral and bacterial—infections that were invisible to us, and would spread like a plague from region to region. We then had a pandemic that engulfed the continent.

It was in these primitive times, circa the eighth century, that the people in the sub-Sahara were visited with a plague that affected the blood cells of my people. The effects of the disease spread mysteriously. Initially it made no exceptions, but that changed quickly. The symptoms were readily apparent: diarrhea, severe stomach pain, and lack of energy. Women were afflicted with an additional discomfort, a lengthy menstruation period with unusually heavy discharge.

Most unusual was how quickly it spread to women—women of all ages. We don't know how it spread. We simply didn't know where it came from. Some people thought it came from tainted wells; some thought it came from eating sick animals.

Our medicine men tried everything they knew, (learned and practiced, up until their time) to fight this new disease of the desert. Their most powerful potions, their herbal remedies, even the most radical drawing of blood, did not work. In the past, these remedies had been successful against other diseases; all proved ineffective against this new blood sickness.

The tribal elders approached the Shaman; you would refer to him as the witch doctor.

The queen laughed and continued.

He knew things no one else knew; he was familiar with *diseases of the blood.*

He told the tribal elders the only medicine that might work is a mixture of oils from the Arabica tree and Pokako juice. It was not easy making the juice. The Shaman ended his comments with, "the potion will either cure the people or kill them."

Clearing her throat, the Queen continued.

We believe the first batch of Pokako juice was made by the witch doctor's father, who, not by design, mixed his semen with the juices of a woman's squirt fluids."

Laughing the Queen said, "We call her the first squirter. We have had our share of crazy doctors. Knowing some of the potions they consumed, I wondered how they stayed alive." She then continued with what she wrote to Dr. Marks.

The elders asked the Shaman to make as much of the toxic juice as was needed to cure the women of our tribe. For unknown reasons, the disease did not affect men in any significant manner. With them, it came, and it went.

The chiefs of the tribe distributed the highly toxic mixture. The toxicity of the juice came from the varying amounts of ureic acid found in the woman's fluids. They gave small quantities of the juice to everyone. Since the blood-invading disease affected mostly women, the elders ordered a larger cup of juice be given to women. This was risky, and they knew it.

The village women took the new juice and to everyone's astonishment, within a matter of weeks, the juice stopped the spread of the disease and began to heal those infected. The Shaman went from village to village to dispense the juice and eventually most of the women were cured—or so we thought. There was a side effect. The juice changed the blood-invasive disease's character and mutated the form of a woman's monthly disorder. The monthly discharge was heavier, and the blood showed more blue coloration than red. This would prove to be significant and with grave consequences, but that would come much later. The women were very happy because they believed they discharged the remnants of the original virulent blood disease, every thirty days.

Generations passed, and the invading blood disease seemed to have vanished as a threat to our region. However, what was not obvious in one generation become obvious after many generations. The elders realized each generation produced fewer children. The overall population of the tribe was in decline.

They realized that the juice's mixture had affected the reproductive organs of women who had taken the juice. Most calamitous was the fact that if a woman had a girl child, it was almost a 100% certain that she too would have the blood disease, known as "sick cell disease" which we call *sickle cell anemia*. The symptoms were clear: stomach pain, difficulty controlling the blood flow during menstruation, loss of appetite and a lack of energy for extended periods. You'll notice these were the same symptoms that first appeared centuries ago."

* * *

If you can find the carrier of the mutated gene and isolate it, you have a chance of eliminating the inevitable progression of future offspring not having any children.

We have to find most, if not all, of the women who carry the mutated gene and give them a regimen of good juice and hope that the antidote will take care of the sickle cell and destroy those cells.

With our current technology, we have been able to sequence the life cycle of the sickle cell through one hundred generations in a month's time. An amazing accomplishment of modern medicine! With just a limited number of subjects, and the addition of the reformulated Pokako juice to the culture containing the sickle cell, we have seen at the end of the 100-generation sequencing, a return to a normal menstrual cycle.

If we can supply the synthetically prepared juice into the African communities, we can eliminate the sickle cell blood disease.

I asked, rather hesitantly, "In laymen's terms, how does the juice effect such dramatic changes.

175

The queen responded, "It appears that the juice, instead of feeding the sickle cells, starves them, and because the cells reproduce fewer and fewer cells, they eventually become too weak to fight our antibodies and 'voila' the sickle cell is eliminated through the menstrual cycle.

"We had to cure the blood disease that the toxic juice developed before we could move on to the juice's true and edifying purpose—the establishment of a world order that will use the knowledge that our past generations created during their enlightened civilizations from the tip of South Africa to the shores of Alexandria."

"Your president is an example of world leadership originating in the bowels of Africa. "His manifesto: A kinder, healthier, sustainable world for all people. That is the mission of the Pokako juice and ours as well."

Women and Weed

How a Baby Boomer Became Involved with the Cannabis Craze

> I will comment just this once that I did smoke weed when I was in college and for a few years thereafter...
>
> —President Bill Clinton

Four years ago, after many years of abstinence, I decided to start smoking again (not cigarettes). The children were grown and gone: taking my wife with them. I was in transition to my "golden years." The future did not have much future; life was boring. So I looked back into my life to find those times that had been exciting for me. The times that came to my mind were the early 80s, when it seemed I danced and smoked every night in some second or third-story loft in

Manhattan's Lower West Side. My odyssey began less than six months afterwards.

On a cool autumn day in the Bronx, a Jamaican friend of mine, via Face Time, introduced me to Tanya. Tanya was going to supply me with an ounce of weed—or, as it is referred to on the street, "a zip." We agreed to meet under the elevated number five train on Westchester Avenue and 165th Street. Tanya was going to sell me a $20.00 bag at a $10.00 price. This way I could roll a joint, try her weed, and see if I liked it. I promised to let her know the following day if I wanted to buy a zip. We met as planned. Five minutes later, I had my weed. Since I was buying for myself and my buddy, Barry, it made sense to stop off at his place and smoke the joint together. Barry was a daily inhaler and could tell good weed from bad. He saw me pull into the driveway and came out to meet me.

"Man, you are crazy," he said. "You go to the South Bronx alone to meet a pot dealer in the evening with money in your pocket? That takes balls and a sincere lack of brainpower."

"I'm here, aren't I? No big deal," I said. I had already taken the weed out and Barry one-handedly began to roll a joint.

"Smells good," he said. We were both anxious about how this street venture would play out. The only way to tell was to smoke the pot. The honor of taking the first hit was mine since I had put my life in "harm's way." I took a deep drag and passed the joint to Barry, who likewise took a deep drag. We did not speak. We just stared at each other like two deer caught in a car's headlights. "This is good shit," I said, smiling ear to ear.

"Yes, I agree," Barry said, as he exhaled his second drag. "We need to get more."

I left Barry and drove home, feeling good and singing along with the Beatles' "Yellow Submarine." Before getting out of the car I tried calling Tanya's number. Why wait until tomorrow? I knew the price; I just had to be sure she didn't pull a switch on me.

"Hi Tanya, it's me," I said, not using my name. "Let's set up a time to meet tomorrow."

"Well, tomorrow," she said, "we have to meet after 9 p.m. I will have a zip for you, but I don't like travelin' on the train with that stuff on me. 'Specially during rush hours. I'm gonna' have somebody with me just to watch my back." I trusted Tanya, and promised to meet her on White Plains Road in the Bronx. At 10 p.m.

I called Barry and told him about the meet. "I will need your share of the money," I said.

"No problem, do you want company?" he asked, half seriously.

"I'll be okay," I answered.

I arrived at the el early. This was intentional. Being early would insure I had a clear view of Tanya and her companion getting off the train platform. Since I drove, I crafted a procedure on how to trade cash for the zip and not leave myself exposed. The best way, I thought, was to be out of the car which would give me space to move, if necessary. Life was getting exciting. However, all of my contingency plans were for naught. The exchange went smoothly. Tanya joined me in the car. As I passed the money to her, her companion passed the zip to me through the driver's window. Tanya counted the money in the car and I weighed the zip. The buds looked good. The oily, resinous texture of the grass felt just right. Tanya was comfortable with the cash as she gave the alright sign to her friend. We kissed on the cheek and said our goodbyes.

Tanya called out: "Go easy. It's strong stuff." I texted Barry to tell him I was safe and would soon be at his place. He was, again, waiting for me in the driveway. As he came closer to me, I threw the zip bag out the window into his arms. "Smells great," he said. "We need to crush the flowers and strain the twigs from the weed. Life is good and getting better."

Tanya and I met a few more times in the fall of 2014. She reminded me of a churchgoing Baptist rather than a dope dealer. She dressed fashionably for the South Bronx. She was not pretty, but sexy. Thin with a small booty in a tight dress. Nice combination. Her teeth gave away the secrets of a hard life. I could sense she wanted better, but with four children and no husband, life will always be hard. We played fair with each other. I knew she would be part of my future.

I found more friends who were also smokers from the 70s. Supplying my baby-boomer friends was not a money producing venture. But I was, unintentionally, building up a client list for later development.

Tanya began to have trouble finding enough product to meet my occasional needs and finally she asked me if I knew any other suppliers that she could tap into. I did not, but a thought began to percolate in my mind. I was spending three hundred on a zip every other month. Was growing out of the question for me? I had some land up the Hudson with a small cabin on the property. It had a well and electricity. My living style was quiet, remote in a way, and I had the internet and YouTube to work with. My biggest concern, I suspected, would be buying good seeds and the best growing soil. The thought of the risks involved was ever present in my mind, but I decided to go ahead anyway.

Once I made the decision to grow my own cannabis, I knew help would be needed. I didn't know anyone with much gardening skill, so I decided I would just have to address that problem later.

My circle of friends, Barry being the exception, would be unable to help me distinguish between okay weed and *I want more of this shit right now* weed. I needed Tanya and her friends from the South Bronx to educate me in how to tell the difference. They grew up with stuff being smoked in the next room, or while strolling with a baby carriage on the way to the supermarket. It was with them from grades one through twelve. They knew good weed; it was in the environmental DNA of the South Bronx. Or, maybe I was just looking for reasons to go and visit Tanya.

One day, as usual, I met her in the South Bronx after 10 p.m. Before 10 she was always taking care of her kids. Her eldest, Melisea, was able to babysit the two younger children, but first Tanya had to put them to bed.

"Baby," she called me, or "honey," or "sweetie," but never by my name. When I was in her neck of the woods, I forgot my name too. Once or twice, I called her sweetie, but mostly I called her Tanya. She liked when I called her by her name. Most of our conversations began with "hey" or "hey, Hon." It was cultural. Here in the Bronx as well as the Caribbean.

"What do you have for me tonight?" I asked.

"Try this," she said, "We call this weed 'Loud.' This is the strongest stuff on the street. There are stronger boutique strains around, but you don't find them on the street."

"If you can't afford to buy Loud, what else can you buy?" I asked.

She laughed and said, "Green is what they sell you. Green grass. The name says it all. It's light stuff."

"Okay, score me some Loud," I said.

"Yeah, I can get you some, but you have to come back tomorrow night. Same time, same place and bring the cash." She leaned over to kiss me goodbye, "Man, you smell so good, so good," she said smiling with her mouth three quarters closed so as not to expose the open spaces between her teeth. I gave her an extra squeeze, just above her booty as I returned her kiss. Her skin was soft to the touch of my lips as I pulled her closer. She ever so slowly turned away and said, "See you tomorrow and remember 'cash is king' down here."

Later that night I lit up a joint. The weed was strong, making me think outside my skin. I knew I had to grow stuff that was popular in the city. There was no sense reinventing the wheel. My customers would pay a handsome price for homegrown, organic, thunder weed.

The winter days were not dull anymore. There was a lot of planning to do. I would need to prepare to be responsible both for the selling and for the growing; from seed, to flower, to product. I would have to supply the muscle when needed. Muscle in the garden, not on the street.

I looked forward to moving up the Hudson and planting my money crop. The cabin was in good shape, and all that was needed was fresh groceries from the local market.

I ordered feminized seeds from a company in Amsterdam. It is the feminine seed that flowers, and it is the flower that contains THC.

The patch of earth that I used for my garden was actually an old run down chicken coop with a fenced-in area to keep the chickens safe when they were out of the coop. The run was loaded with chicken shit and it had direct sun for most of the day. A perfect location for my "Lady" plants.

The first month after germination is the most critical. This is the time when you transfer the seedling to a small degradable pot and hope all goes well. Two weeks after, you transfer the young seedling into a well fertilized watered hole with enough minerals to keep the plant healthy for the next two months. The plants would go through a growth stage and then a flowering stage.

So far I had been lucky. I had correctly chosen the days to go up, when I needed to be there, and had had no surprises.

But after four weeks the plants were now in their growth stage, and they required more attention. Reading cannabis magazines gave me a clearer picture of the complete growing cycle. I decided to stay at the cabin for the duration of the growing season and through the harvest.

Staying at the cabin gave me time to check the plants twice a day. It's best to water in the morning, before the sun can dry the soil.

One morning, lost in thought as I examined the plants, I heard a voice coming from the driveway about fifty yards from the coop. "Hello, hello," she said. "Anybody up yet?"

I didn't want to expose the coop to strangers or, for that matter, to anybody other than Tanya. I could see it was a woman, a black woman. I jogged over to meet her before she got onto the field.

"Hi," I said, "can I help you?"

"Hi," she responded in a musical Caribbean accent, "I am the au pair to your neighbor's newborn baby down the road. I am staying with the Brady family. My name is Zena. Every day that it doesn't rain, I walk little Brady Jr. past your driveway until the road gives way to the hill which is too hard for me to push the pram, so I turn me and the little man baby around and pass your home for the second time."

I smiled. "I find it difficult myself getting up that hill with my car. But it's good exercise for you."

She laughed. "During the past week, the weather was beautiful, as you know; I was able to smell the flowers that you are growing. It should come as no surprise to you, that coming from Jamaica, I know what you are growing." She laughed in that Jamaican way, the laugh coming from deep down in her belly. "I want to help you in the garden." She continued, "I grew ganja in Jamaica, and I will be a good helper when it comes to harvesting and preparing your plants for drying."

"Where do you live in the city?"

"I live on 165th Street in the South Bronx," she replied.

I laughed. "That's funny. The only other person I know in the Bronx that lives on 165th Street is a woman whose name is Tanya."

"OMG, OMG, Tanya lives in my building. She sells good weed. Is that your stuff she be sellin'?"

"It will be," I said.

"Is it just business, or are you doin' her?" she asked with this slight smile, but more with a devil's look in her eyes.

I laughed again. "For now, it's just business. Do you mind if I visit the Baileys in the next few days to congratulate them on their new joy and to get an idea of how they feel about your helping me?"

Zena smiled, "That is a nice way to check up on me. I appreciate how cautious you have to be. No problem; do you have their telephone number?"

"Yes I do. I will call John later."

When she reached the paved driveway, Zena turned, smiled, waved, and said, "See you later."

Well, that was interesting, I thought. I was not sure how I felt about Zena. I was sure she would be a big help, but she would also be a distraction. Zena was young, pretty, and dark skinned with big lips, beautiful brown eyes that looked almost black, big breasts, a great smile, and of course, the perfect Nubian booty.

Thinking about having Zena around, I realized the gardening help I needed had just dropped in my lap. I had been unsure whether my absence of a few days every other week would affect the growth of the plants. With Zena here, that would not be an issue. It would be comforting to have somebody cover for me when I had to travel back to the city. I laughed; it looked like I had already made up my mind about Zena.

Now I could daydream about both Tanya and Zena. Here's to mountain air, women, and weed. This aging transition could be very exciting.

Zena was true to her word. She knew how to take care of cannabis plants, and I guess any other life form that grows in the garden. One day, as we were preparing the shed for hanging and drying our plants, she told me what she

187

had done in Jamaica during the last stage of the ganja flowering period.

"Now, Mr. Grower," she laughed, "you will not believe this, and you may not like what I am going to suggest we do, but in my country, at this time, we make sure these plants will have big flowers and big leaves. Bigger than what you see now."

I looked at Zena suspiciously. "Okay, okay, what do you do?"

"Mr. Grower, you and I will urinate on the plants which gives them a shot of urea, very rich in nitrogen. It is very important to do at this stage. We will then water the plants to dilute the urine and you will have a very good harvest!"

I looked at Zena and said, "That is something that I would do—if I were crazy."

"No, no, *mon,* you are not crazy; we call it the golden harvest."

I just started to laugh. "We have an old American Indian tradition that tells how the women would rub the oils of their breasts against the leaves of the corn plants. Why don't you try rubbing your breasts against the cannabis leaves? I see the oil drops coalescing between your breasts right now."

Zena was not laughing. She said, "How do you know about that? How do you know we do that in Jamaica too?"

"Are you serious?" I said. "It was an old wives' tale. We won't do that. However, I believe in the science of urea and I know it will be good for the plants. So, let's pee."

I showed her where the water pans were that I used to use to supply water to the chickens. "I am going to get a notebook. Wait for me to return. I want to know which plants will receive the hyper nitrogen." I must be nuts! I thought. But, this was all about a fabulous harvest, and if I could get a better yield both in quantity and quality, then I was game. It was simple; we were adding more nitrogen via urea. Nothing more.

Zena got the water pan, and I went to the cabin to get the notebook. When I returned, Zena was waiting for me. The water pan was half full with the golden yellow liquid. I handed her a six-ounce plastic cup and told her to use one cup for each plant.

"I will be behind you with the hose. No chance of acid burn to the plants."

"There is not enough urine in the pan for all the plants. It is your turn, Mr. Grower," she said.

"Why do you call me 'Mr. Grower'? We are not on a plantation in Jamaica. We are up in the mountains along the Hudson with two beautiful lakes on either side of this mountain. The air is pure and sweet smelling and it's hot during the day and cool in the evening. The temperature seems to be thermostatically controlled by the prevailing westerly winds. Why plantation images?"

"Because," she said, "I can see that you like the nobility of being the grower. Now, you may not like this, but it is your turn to pee into the pan." She handed me a pan, laughing, and waiting to see what I would do.

Looking at the plants and then at the pan and visualizing the image of what I was going to do brought out the Brooklyn in me. I took off my pants, dropped my underwear and started to direct my pee onto the roots of each plant. This is what I would do in Brooklyn if I had a garden. As I moved around I had to get out of my underwear because my feet were getting caught.

Zena could not stop laughing. "What a cute small ass you have," she sang out. "Has me hometown woman seen your cute ass?"

"No, Tanya has not seen me naked," which I now was. I finished adding my liquid to the plants and turned to find my shorts. Much to my surprise, Zena was now naked as well. The first thought that crossed my mind was an image of a black naked Madonna whose beauty had been shaped over the last million years, standing an arm's length from me.

"You like?" she asked, spreading her arms out from her side to form an inverted "V" with her body.

"Yes, I like very much. Especially your bikini wax. But this is not the time for us to like each other. I want to wait until we harvest our crop and then we can celebrate. I will not forget this moment. In fact, I think I will have many dreams about it."

"You are a strong-willed man, Mr. Grower. I too will not forget your shape, both front and back. Can I tell Tanya about this wonderful morning?" she asked.

"Of course," I said. "But, tell her the truth," I was trying to be serious, but not succeeding in the least, as we both burst out laughing.

"I will be very serious and honest, my Mr. Grower."

"You should go home; it is getting late. I will see you on Sunday." We kissed, very softly, and I said, "I can't wait to see you." Then we put our clothes back on.

Tanya sent me a text asking how I was doing and when was I coming back to the Bronx, and was the "*stuff*" ready, and she wanted to talk to me 'bout something.' I thought what she really meant to say was, "Hon, I miss you, when are you comin' back?" I wanted to tell her about Zena, and see if she already knew about my new friend and helper. *When it rains it pours.*

Who would think that growing weed upstate on a rural piece of land, surrounded by nothing of importance, I would find romance, passion and lust! Just like my college days in Brooklyn. But, I reminded myself, the idea was to grow weed, not fall in love with two beautiful women. *I must concentrate on the plants!* I repeated to myself. The flowering stage had begun, and I had to watch for leaf rot, flower mites, and mineral deficiencies. Zena would be here later. We'd begin cleaning out the low-lying stems from the area near the trunk of the plant. These stems do not get enough sun to produce flowers. They are always in the shadow of the leaves on top which spread out and block the daylight.

Keeping track of time was becoming harder; there were long hot days followed by nights with lots of stars. I lost all focus on what day it was.

Sunday felt like a Friday, but it was Sunday. I was sure. It was a lazy day, and I did not feel like getting to the garden before noon. It did not matter much as Zena always came after two. Today, she arrived a little after three. I was already on my knees checking for bugs and moisture content of the soil.

"You know nothing, Mr. Grower, about weed growin'. But you are not afraid to try different possibilities. I like that about you," was her after-noon greeting.

Not even a hello or good afternoon. "Why do you say that?" I asked.

"Because, I can see you are a businessman and not a farmer."

"I know that. But if I'm to make money, I need to learn how to grow this form of hemp. Do you find me lazy, weak of character, or ignorant?" I asked her.

"No, you have good character. Most men would have stopped tryin' to learn about growin,' and would not listen to me. You need me, Mr. Grower, and I need you, in ways that you don't understand. Yet."

"Are we still talking about farming?"

Zena looked at me for a long moment, and I responded in kind. It seemed it was a matter of who would blink first. I admit, I laughed first, and then she laughed as well.

"My god, Zena, the sex will be wonderful."

"Yes. We must make love in the field next to the garden and be stoned too. *Comprende*?"

She took my hand and put my fingers in her mouth. I could feel the electricity shooting to all parts of my body. Sensual, but unsanitary. Yet I didn't want to stop her.

"We must be getting a contact high standing in the coop surrounded by all of our hemp plants," I said. "Zena! We are getting high," I repeated.

"Yes, I think so too."

"Do you want to take a swim in the lake? It's just over the ridge," I asked.

"Yes, I would like that; I have wanted to take a swim in that lake since we came up from the city. I want to swim naked," she added. "It's so private here; it reminds me of my school days in Ocho Rios."

We were standing very close to each other when she turned her body to give me her booty side. She wiggled a little so that we fit well together. I moved in to remove any unwanted space.

"You like my booty, Mr. Grower?"

"Yes, I love your booty," I said as I slid both my hands on her ass to reinforce my admiration. Judging by her wiggle, she was certainly on the same wavelength.

"I am glad this is Sunday; I don't have to leave until later," she whispered in my ear.

"Don't you think it is time that you call me John?" I asked.

"I do not like 'John'; I prefer to call you 'sweetie,' or 'honey,' but not 'John.' I like 'Jonnie Grower.' 'Grower,' it sounds personal. I want to call you by a name that nobody else uses. You are special, we are special, and our Mary Janes are special."

"What about your name?" I asked.

"Have you ever heard or talked to a Zena before?" she replied.

"Okay, point made," I responded, not wanting to get into a pissing contest with her.

"Let's go swimming while it's still light." I said. "However, first things first, I have a confession of sorts to make before we are locked in each other's naked arms."

Zena had that "oh my god here comes terrible news" expression on her face.

I continued, "I contracted a desert virus during the first Iraq war. It affected my sexual libido. The doctors thought it might be dengue fever. But that was just a guess. They never found out what it was; however, to keep both of us happy during sex, I need to take a pill. The pill keeps me hard for quite a while."

"My sweetie, you don't have to take a chemical to make love with me. I will bring you to that special place in your body and mind without the blue pill."

"Maybe, but the pill is a guarantee that all will work well for me, for us. I will be hard for a long time. Think of it as if I were taking an Aleve. Both are blue."

"Grower, you are a funny man. Ok, how much time do we have to wait before the pill starts to work?"

"I took the pill a while ago; we don't have to wait at all."

"You want me! You care for me!" she called to the heavens as she danced and sang in her sing-song, Jamaican, *mon* accent.

"Now, can we go to the lake?"

"Yes, we can go," she said, as she kissed me lightly on the lips.

We held hands as we climbed to the top of the hill. She squeezed my hand, and we crested the top. Gosh, it was beautiful. I knew Zena felt the same way. The lake was spread out in front of us, like a fan. It was radiant blue and pacific, inviting us to join and play in her while the late afternoon sun still had power.

I loved that Zena's emotions were so transparent. She said what she wanted to say without filter. A squeeze of my hand spoke of her feelings without saying a word. I was losing myself in the fantasy of love, romance, and passion. Today, I was in love. That was all I could wish for.

My long-sleeved shirt served as a blanket. I spread it out on the soft grass closest to the water (I always tend my garden with an extra-large, long shirt to protect myself from insect bites).

Zena wore less and was undressed before I finished straightening out my shirt.

Again, she assumed the "V" to show me her beautiful brown body.

"Take your pants off, my sexy farmer, or would you like me to take them off for you?"

"I would love that," I said as I lay down on my shirt. I already had an erection which Zena saw as she approached me.

"Look at my Grower! You are already there. I thought I would have to work and use all the techniques I know to get you hard."

She was talking as she took my pants off. *How lucky,* I thought, *a woman who could multitask.*

"You are so beautiful. I don't know where to begin," I said.

"Begin? Anywhere you like, just begin!" She laughed with her deep belly laugh. "Kiss me, kiss me hard." She brought her lips to mine, followed by her body on top of mine. She adroitly placed my statue so as not to break it between her legs. I could feel her juices running down my inner thighs. She was correct. She had all the technique necessary to revive the nearly dead. Without missing a beat, she lifted herself onto me and in a thrust I was in her.

She took all of me.

"Keep growing inside of me," she whispered as she came down hard on me. Zena was strong enough to lift her body off me a good six inches and then drop hard on my loins. Again and again; we never separated.

Life didn't get any better. At that moment, I was at the high point of my mortal existence, no longer on earth, somewhere else. I didn't know where, nor did I care. It was our time to give thanks to Mother Nature, which we did in many different ways.

We did not speak for quite a while. I held Zena as tightly as I could without hurting her. I wanted to take care of her and protect her. I felt like a conqueror who had vanquished his enemy and won the Queen's heart.

"Grower, I really like what you have between your legs. Can I take it home with me?" she asked, again laughing with that deep belly laugh.

"My sweetie, it's yours. If I could loan it to you for a while and then get it back, I would do that." Now we both laughed as she gently kissed the head of my statue and made it taller.

"Oh Mr. Grower, I want more Jamaican luvin'. This place is too beautiful to waste and you taste so good."

"Jamaican luvin', what's that?" I asked.

"I show you," she said as she slowly lifted her legs and straddled my head.

Just as she began to move onto my face, the rains came—more accurately, thunderstorms— big drops. They hurt. We began running like hell to get back to my cabin. Suddenly, Zena stopped. She wanted to walk and hold my hand. Rain be damned, it was only water. We dried off in the cabin and I suggested I take her back to the Bailey house. I sensed her anxiety and nervous-ness about that suggestion.

"Is there anything going on with you and Mr. Bailey?" I asked.

"No, but I think he would like there to be something."

"Let's talk about Mr. Bailey later. There are more important issues that we have to discuss. This is not a lecture. In fact, as I am talking to you, I am instructing myself as well. The next two weeks are critical. We can't—I repeat: we can't—forget our shared responsibilities.

"The plants are in the flowering stage and we have to be diligent and not take any short-cuts. Plant food and water must be our mantra until we complete harvesting. Zena, rolling in the grass with you is a pure delight, but it's not why I am here. I, and now you—we—are here to grow weed and then sell the weed. To make lots of money; plain and simple.

"Somehow, I think it's more than just blind luck that you came into my life at this time. You are talented, and you understand what needs to be done. I'll be here at 7 a.m. for the next two weeks."

Zena, thankfully, answered as I'd hoped she would: "I can come at 7 a.m. for a few hours and then again at 4 p.m. every day this week. Mrs. Bailey will be home the whole week. Her company is closed for summer vacation."

The next morning, I arrived at the garden a little after sunrise. I was getting nervous. We were into the homestretch. The smell was much stronger. A good sign of health for the plants.

I made my final count of healthy, flowering plants. Originally, I had planted forty, but I'd lost a few during the transplant and now had thirty-seven left. Mentally, I was calculating the potential yield in ounces from each plant.

As I daydreamed about this, I noticed an odd flowering configuration on one of the plants. The buds were smaller and shaped like peas. They were smooth skinned and circular, in clusters, with little of the traditional bud formation. Something bothered me about this growth pattern.

Later, I went onto YouTube and searched. The answers I found were chilling: "You have a male plant ready to release its pollen!" I knew that if the male plant pollinated the female plants we would have seeds, not weed colas to harvest.

It was nine o'clock in the evening now. I jumped off the computer and grabbed a flashlight. I knew what I had to do, and I had to do it immediately.

Thankfully, there was a full moon that night so I didn't break my neck running to the chicken shed. In the shed I looked for the male plant and examined it to see if it had begun to pollinate. Not yet—the pods were still intact. It was hard to pull the plant out of the ground. I used a sharply filed shovel to get the roots out.

They were deep and had spread a good twelve inches off the main trunk. Care had to be taken not to disturb the root systems of the surrounding plants.

Next I dragged the plant out of the shed area and cut it into little pieces. They would be good compost. It was hard work. The plant's root system with its ball of earth was heavy. I was tired, but very happy that I'd discovered the male plant when I did. I had purchased only feminized seeds. No male or hybrid seeds. Shit happens. I decided to say nothing to Zena when I saw her the next day. We had a very good crop coming into flower and I didn't want to worry her. She understood she had a payday coming. This was a close call. I hoped I wouldn't have nightmares about this incident.

With Zena able to come a few hours in the early morning, we began to harvest the mature plants. I bought a bag of one hundred plastic surgical gloves to keep the oils from the flowers off our hands. The oil was almost viscous, and it stuck to everything. The scissors would have to be soaked and cleaned in alcohol every day. We hung clotheslines in the shed. Slowly we began to pull up plants that were in full bloom. At first there were only two, which was fine, as it gave us the opportunity to organize our future production schedule. It also allowed me to estimate, roughly, the yield from those first two plants.

My scale was an accurate one that measured to the tenths of a gram. I weighed the colas (a bunch of bud clusters) of the first plant and calculated how many colas we could expect from each plant. Taking into account the drying period, I anticipated a yield of 16 ounces, or 500 grams—a little over a pound. A hypothetical street value of $6,000 a plant. At 37 plants, that would net 200k-plus on the street. Selling to distributers would bring us 125k at one time. Let *them* make the other 100k selling on the street. Tanya will be very happy, I thought.

Tanya had been preparing her distributers for this harvest. They knew how good the weed was from last winter's tasting. The yield would make her very comfortable financially. And if we could repeat the harvest over the next three summers, we should both have enough to live comfortably, assuredly, for the rest of our lives. Under these circumstances I would have very little selling to do. Except to my "boomer" friends.

Time passes quickly when you're having fun. Not surprisingly, Zena and I couldn't keep our hands off each other. We found a spot under a tree where the shade of the tree kept the grass short and dry. I kept a blanket in the shed for just those times.

Every now and then, while lying next to me, Zena would ask, "Grower, are you coming to see me when I go back to the city?"

"Yeah, I think I will be spending a lot of time in the South Bronx."

"But will you be coming to see *me*? And will you bring me with you next summer? Even if I don't have the nanny job?"

"One question at a time," I responded. I knew what she wanted to hear, but I didn't want to say too much yet. I knew that Zena would be with me wherever I ended up. Unless it was jail.

"Zena, did you tell Tanya about us? Please tell me you didn't?"

"No, I didn't tell Tanya. Why do you say that?"

"Because she sent me a text, which I immediately erased from my phone, but I think she knows."

"OMG, Mr. Bailey must have said something to her."

"Why would Mr. Bailey say something to Tanya? Why and how would he even know her?" I shouted.

Zena replied, half crying, "Because she supplies Mr. Bailey with his weed and his... other stuff."

"Are you telling me that Bailey is an addict?"

"Yes, and Tanya was tryin' to keep him on soft stuff, like weed."

"Okay, let's start from the beginning. How much does Tanya know about us?"

Zena smiled and said, "She knows you're a good lay," again, laughing with her deep belly laugh.

"Stop fooling around—this is serious. Does Bailey know what I am doing here? Is he doing Tanya?"

"That's a funny question coming from you," she said with a twinkle in her eyes.

"How long has Tanya been helping Bailey?"

"I don't know! But long enough for her to get me this job for the summer."

I had never bothered to ask Zena about her background or how long she had been working for the Baileys. This was certainly a breach of security.

"Zena, how *did* you get this summer job? Tanya hardly knows you."

"I know, but I helped her out one day when her regular babysitter was drunk, and I took her youngest with me to my apartment. I thought it would be safer for the kid. Tanya was very grateful to me for helping her. She knew I was a responsible person, and they are not easy to come by in the South Bronx."

"Does Bailey's wife know about his drug problem and his friendship with Tanya?"

Zena looked at me and said, "I don't know what all Mrs. Bailey knows. I think the baby was an accident. I can tell by the way Mrs. Bailey talks about Mr. Bailey and about Bailey Jr. And

I think Tanya is going to visit sometime this week."

"Why would you think that?"

"Jonnie Farmer, you are asking a lot of questions today."

"You must have some other information that would lead you to that conclusion."

"You're so smart! You're too smart to be a farmer. You'd be a good detective. I got a text from her yesterday as well, asking me about the weather and shit like that."

"If you have the facilities to take her child in, am I to assume that you have a child as well?"

"Yes I do," she responded.

"Well, obviously, I'm not smart enough. This is a mess. I can't ask Mr. Bailey to allow you to help me. He probably knows what I am growing and I don't want to put you in a position of having to lie to him. So, let's forget about Sundays from now on. Just help me in the evening when his wife is at home and she can watch both of them at the same time. It's Tanya I am worried about. But first, let's finish learning more about you. I don't want any more surprises. Are you in this country legally?"

"Yes, the father of my child is an American and my child was born here. I have a green card and in three years I will be a citizen," she proudly volunteered.

"Do you have any idea what day Tanya will be coming up?"

"It will be a Tuesday or Wednesday. Those are the days she usually has a babysitter. I think she's out for business on those days."

"Good, I checked the weather for tomorrow and it is supposed to rain all day, so we will not meet tomorrow. Do you know if Tanya has a car?"

"No, I don't think so, but she does drive. I know she rents a car to go to see her family in Jersey and another part of her family in Brooklyn."

I was worried. I didn't want to tell Zena, but what I had thought was to be a vacation of sorts for me (with the appropriate amount of profitable outdoor labor) had turned into a dissonance of conflict between the participants: the Baileys and their marriage, his addiction, her reluctance to accept their child, and their relationship with Tanya, and my relationship with Zena and hers with Tanya. A real shit-storm.

Tanya and I would have a lot to talk about when she came up. I knew she would be pissed. My head hurt. It was time to smoke some product, drink some wine, and, hopefully, just pass out and wake up to a rainy Monday. There were a couple of good things about this. One, I didn't have to water the plants. Two, I didn't have to get out of bed. No visitors; no problems!

Tuesday, according to the local newspaper, would be a beautiful day. I wondered if I should prepare the cabin for a visitor. On second thought, I didn't think Tanya would be receptive to any after-hour activities.

Tuesday was as nice as they'd said it would be. The rains had left very early in the morning. I was sure the plants had grown a good couple of inches over the last two days. Rain followed by sunshine will make any grower look good. My walk to the garden confirmed the growth spurt of my ladies.

"Hello, hello, anyone home on this God-forsaken hill?" someone shouted. I recognized Tanya's Bronx accent immediately.

"I'm over here, Tanya—just follow the sound of my voice or the smell of the weed. Both will lead you to the Promised Land," I shouted back.

"Well, well, so here you are. Promised Land, my ass! You're a fuckin' idiot. Stupid! Stupid, like all men, you been thinkin' with your dick. You're just a piece of shit. You jeopardized our whole winter's business for some fresh pussy. You piece of shit! Bailey is my money man and indirectly yours. He funds my buys. And you fuck his babysitter. Nice! You piece of shit," she growled.

"I expect this type of bullshit from my street-grown brothers, but not from a white guy who has stuff. You're just like my brothers. One thing, and one thing only, on your minds. How did you last so long in this world? Bein' so stupid?

"I sent Zena up here to help you and to watch over Mr. Bailey. She's no different than the rest of those imports from Jamaica. Show me the money! I thought you would be different. I like you and thought we could make a go of it.

"My god, if you had waited until we finished our business, I would have gladly taken you as my man and we would have made a good twosome. In business and in bed. I wouldn't have minded if Zena joined us, what the hell, she's young, sweet, and plump, ready for the squeezing and pickin' so why shouldn't you have a go," she smiled and continued.

"I was at the dentist this week getting my mouth measured for new teeth. So I can smile, an' we can go dancing in Harlem. We would look fancy, you in black tux and I in a white body suit."

I laughed until I was light-headed. Tanya laughed, too, and behind the bushes I thought I heard Zena's laugh as well.

"Tanya, I'm sorry I disappointed you. You're right; I can't keep my zipper closed. It just happened. I didn't know that you sent Zena to help me. Besides planting and harvesting this summer, I had one thought that I kept ever present in my mind. This was to bring back thirty-five pounds of the best Loud money would buy. I can see you with new teeth, new house, and good schools for your kids."

Tanya interjected, "Next year, we bring back fifty pounds."

"Absolutely," I shouted to the heavens.

I knew that my financial comfort was due in no small part to the sacrifice that Tanya had made this year in selling most of the harvest to distributors. She would've made a lot more money if she had taken the time to sell the production through her people on the street. I didn't want to hold on to the crop and have to package the proceeds in ounce zips. The answer to "how a baby boomer became a cannabis dealer" was not a simple or a straightforward one. And people always complicate the process.

This summer had also been a life changer for Zena. Somewhere, she must've picked a handful of four-leaf clovers because she struck gold when she stumbled into my "field of dreams."

"My dream was to drive a racing green BMW convertible with you and Zena in the car—driving slowly down Broadway and smoking a hand-rolled joint," I said to Tanya.

"Honey, I'll share that dream with you if you let me drive."

"Hell, Tanya, with the money we make, I see two convertibles in our future. Isn't it true that two B'mers are cheaper than one?"

"Life is smelly and messy. Your sense of smell will tell you whether you're smellin' a fragrance or an odor. It's nice when you can combine the two and come up with perfume. Get my drift?"

Tanya smiled with a wide open mouth—probably, the last time I would see her smiling with a few of her teeth missing.

The nights were now longer, and the days had that autumn feel about them. The change in weather brought a new reality to our small group. Dreams were just that—dreams.

It was time to harvest the Mary Janes. This was our first harvest. It went well but not without its headaches. We suffered the loss of three plants to bud rot and two plants to worm fungus. The bud rot and the fungus were the result of an unusually rainy September. Unfortunately, Zena had to leave a few days earlier than expected as her son was accepted into a very highly acclaimed pre-school program. The cleaning and packaging took a few days longer without her. The Baileys left the farm and returned to the city almost a month earlier than expected. Rumor had it that they were headed into divorce court and they would not be coming back to their farm next summer. The fall came and left, followed by the winter. Winter stayed with us a little longer than expected. Tanya earned enough money to complete her move out of the South Bronx and into Yonkers. Zena packed her belongings, and she too left the Bronx and moved to Yonkers. I was the only person to buy a BMW. It was obvious they had more important things to buy with their money. We did not get as much money as we hoped for. The Californians had flooded the market with inexpensive weed, which was actually quite good. And, if truth be told, by the time I dried and cured the weed we lost two pounds of weight (water weight), which was to be expected. But, with all the obstacles, we still did quite well.

Along the way, I became a sugar daddy, mentor, and lover to both Tanya and Zena. Amazingly, I had found a new career in my middle age. I had to admit life was exciting and rewarding. I felt important in a way I had not felt before. Despite having purely selfish motives, I was helping a few *other* people lead a better life. I enjoyed tasting new foods of the Caribbean, especially Jamaican Oxtail Stew. Zena filled me in on some of the less well-known customs of the women of Jamaica. She told me many stories of her life there, stories rich with information about the customs and mores of the West Indies. She also told me why she would never invite her mom to have dinner with us. She called her mom a *man stealer*. That was why, she told me, "Mr. Grower, you'll never meet my mom."

And I never did.

Tanya, although busy with her new home and neighborhood, could not wait for the next growing season to begin.

"Mr. Grower, when are you going to take a ride up to your favorite chicken coop and make sure it's still standing?"

"Tanya, my love, I will go up the first week in March and bring supplies to the farm as needed. I know you have concerns, but we have time. Everything will be in order for the growing season."

"Have you made arrangements for additional help? Because I *ain't supplyin' women* for you this time."

"Tanya, I'm okay. Thanks for looking out for me." I didn't tell her that I had already asked Zena to come up and help me. I didn't think she would be pleased.

For the first time in my life I had enough money to cover my responsibilities, and enough loving to make me feel I would stay young forever. I don't know if these are my golden years, but, if you ask me, I would say so.

Good weed, a fast car, great sex, and a young kid (Zena's) who looked up to me. He even calls me grandpa!

The next two months were spent getting the cabin cleaned up and adding a few pieces of furniture that I thought would make Zena more comfortable during the next growing season.

At the same time, Zena had completed her move back to the Bronx in the Pelham section to be closer to her extended family. As she told me, "I like to hear Jamaican music and eat jerk chicken sandwiches. I can't do that in Yonkers." Target and BJ's were her go-to stores for most of her needs. The Caribbean food markets of the Bronx supplied her with specialty foods which always brought back memories of her childhood in Jamaica.

Besides, her son's grandmothers lived there. They loved to take care of him and walk him to and from school every day.

Our second harvest had a lot riding on it. Tanya was planning to take Cyrus, the father of three of her children, into her home to become her business partner once he'd finished a brief jail stay. (Her other baby's father was not around.) She would need plenty of good product to keep them both busy.

Cyrus was the father of other children as was the prevailing custom among many West Indian communities. He had had run-ins with the law, but he was not a felon; he'd just gotten wrapped up in a legal system that put you in jail when you couldn't pay a fine. As he explained to Tanya, "I owed a fifty-dollar parking ticket, but by the time I got the notices and appeared in court I owed $250 for the ticket and $275 for the cost of the court. In Texas anything over $500 is an automatic six months in jail."

What it sounded like to me was a repeat of debt servitude. Our present penal system dates back to the English system of centuries ago. We just gave it a new name: "Justice."

Tanya was, if anything, a realist. She needed help raising her four children. Having to go out to work every day, she needed someone she could trust with them. With Cyrus at home, she would not have to beggar for help.

The word *trust* had a different connotation in their community. It was used in the context of life or death. It far exceeded the gravity of "I trust you will take care of yourself," which is how a father would have used it when talking to his son. There is an absence of true danger implied in the father's words.

Life had been tough for Tanya. She had been raised by her mother, and only vaguely remembered her father. It had been easier for her mom to get government aid if she lived alone than if her babies' daddy lived with them. The welfare system seemed to believe that fathers who didn't work had no other reason to live with the family. "My mom could've fixed my teeth. It was free when I was in the second grade. Because she didn't, I didn't smile for many years."

I asked her where she'd grown up and her answer was "all over." That was the end of the conversation. Her early years showed the harm that a dysfunctional family can do to children. It formed, for her, clarity of purpose: she understood the importance of Cyrus being a part of the household.

Tanya kept her personal life separate from her businesses. I knew she would not alter that. She had her piece of the pie and simply wanted to maintain it. All I had to do with Tanya was keep her in weed to sell, and she would be satisfied.

She began all of her conversations with "What's next?" "What's next, Mr. Grower? We need to plant more Sour Diesel. My people can't get enough of it. Why are you planning to plant other strains when everyone is asking for SD?"

"Because variety is the spice of life and, more importantly, it is beneficial to the soil to vary the seeds that we plant."

Zena was in a different space. She was a member of the next generation of immigrants from the Caribbean, which came to New York having completed their primary schooling. So she had finished high school and completed her associates' certification in nursing already.

"Old man," she would say, when she wasn't calling me "Mr. Grower, I have big plans for the future. I'll be a registered nurse before I'm thirty and working with you will give me the business experience I need to sell real estate. That's where the money will come from: the big money.

As the weeks passed, she shared more and more of her life with me: "My baby's father wants to take me to court and take custody of my baby. The judge is gonna' laugh him out of court. He has no job, lives with his mom, just fathered another out-of-wedlock baby girl, and he's hangin' out with high school girls. I want to make sure the judge sees me as a successful responsible young woman and shuts this case down for good."

How could I not want to take Zena with me for the next growing season? I needed her. The Jamaican ganja plants were not easy to cultivate, and her skills with them had been essential the summer of the first harvest. Besides, the whirling dervish of sex kept me young and fresh all winter.

The snows in February kept us apart for longer periods than usual. I could sense the tension that day we met. She was always wet and would take me to bed every day if I could and would. Our tryst that afternoon was like non-fiction fantasy. There I was, lying between her legs, thinking how to confuse her flowerhead into looking for the frenzy and excitement of just a minute ago. The bud grew in my mouth, it searched for the trigger to recreate the speed and slashing of my tongue. All the while, her mind and body prepared for a last major assault from my intrusive tongue.

"Use your finger, wet it first and stick it as deeply as you can in my ass. Faster! Faster!" Zena began now speaking in some ancient Jamaican language. I heard her moan, "Mother, mother," and then her legs began to shiver and clamp down hard around my ears. "Say my name," I whispered into her pussy.

"Mr. Grower, Jonny Grower," she moaned. At that moment, with my last inhale I blew all the air across her clit. My breath was hot, very hot. Her twisted body was waiting for this signal.

"Oh my God, stop! Stop! Don't touch me. I'm like a ripe tomato, another squeeze and I will burst. I have already seeded your eyes, mouth, and nose. I cannot stop *orgasming.* I have no control. You may be an old man, but you're my old man."

Then there was her unbridled self-confidence, especially when she didn't know what she was talking about. Driving, for instance.

"Turn here, honey, right turn, turn," she would demand, her voice going up a couple hundred decibels.

"Zena, I was on the wrong side of the road."

"You don't listen. I think you don't hear me! You could have turned."

"Honey, I hate to tell you, you know very little about driving. Why you insist on instructing me remains a mystery. However, you do make me laugh. A lot."

"Yeah, I notice you're always laughing when I try to give you good advice. Why are you always laughing?"

"Because you insist on giving me orders when you know I pay no attention to them," I said to her. "Yet you continue, and I find that very funny. I guess if I didn't laugh, we would be fighting all the time."

"Wait until I get my driver's license," Zena retorted.

"When you get your license I will stay out of the Bronx for the first six months."

"Why would you do that?"

"Because I don't want to get into an accident with you, much less any car-to-car shouting matches." With that, we would both started laughing.

Zena had a whole list of things she wouldn't do: wear hand-me-down clothing, use somebody else's toothbrush, eat red meat or tomatoes, and she wouldn't eat in a restaurant without inspecting her silver and glassware. She always pressed her uniform before going to work and took long, very long, showers. She treated herself to a new sex toy every few months. I was included in her coven of sex toys.

Until I met Zena, I had never spent time with a truly narcissistic person. She could not pass up any chance she got to admire herself and did not attempt to disguise the love she had for the mirror. Of course, she was *almost* always right. She had all the right beauty aids, weight-reducing belts, exercise tapes, and clothing to maintain and accentuate her breasts and her booty.

"Keep on exercisin' ole man," she would say. I loved it when she teased me. In fact, I would do whatever she wanted me to (except when it came to driving). I could not wait to spend a whole summer with her.

I had more than a passing personal admiration for Zena. She brought me back from the ten-yard line to midfield, so to speak. Repeatedly, unknowingly, she helped me resist life's assaults, as they pushed me closer to their end where, as you know, once you cross the line, the game was over.

Mostly, I liked taking her journey with her as long as she allowed me to. Love comes in many shapes and forms. The passionate times of lying together and making love began to taper off quite naturally. As I said to her, "We are like older married couples that have reached the point where having sex is not the most critical element of our relationship."

She laughed and said, "It certainly feels like that." To me that was a sign that we were friends and cared for each other beyond the bedroom.

The sale of her home in Yonkers had given her enough money to buy a nice apartment in the Pelham area and send Ramon to a highly rated private pre-K school. Then she was house rich and cash poor. I stepped in, making sure she had enough money to buy him school clothes and a sharp looking and rather unusual Nike kid's winter coat. We picked Ramon up together almost every day during his first months of school. From there, usually, we went to Kentucky Fried, where I bought his chicken and mashed potatoes dinner. Zena added all kinds of West Indian vegetables to his dish; right next to the potatoes. Ramon ate healthy and well.

Zena was an excellent nurse's assistant, but her pay was modest. In six months, she would join the union and get benefits and a higher pay rate. Meanwhile, although there were times that I needed my money as badly as she did—I was carrying two homes, two cars, and all the expenses that come with them—I made sure that Zena had enough money to get on the subway and get to work every day.

I was so proud when she asked me to accompany her shopping and help her buy a winter coat. She wanted and valued my opinion. I just had to abide by her golden shopping rules: "Don't try to hold my hand, and don't try to kiss me or touch me suggestively," she cautioned, laughing in her melodic Jamaican accent. It made sense, given the obvious difference in our ages. I selected a long sexy, brand-named coat with a faux fur collar.

The coat fit well and was warm. She looked good in it. It showed off her booty, but not too much. The length made her look slimmer and taller. "I love it!" she exclaimed. It seemed as if she stopped in front of every mirror in the store. I think her friends were going to be quite envious of her. Knowing Zena, she couldn't wait to flaunt, with flair, her new garb.

Repeatedly, Zena told me how important Tanya was to the success of last year's harvest.

"I like and respect Tanya. She's been through the street wars and survived to raise a family, and she's a very good businesswoman."

I agreed. Tanya was irreplaceable.

However they did it, both women were on their way to achieving the American dream.

I hoped I'd be here, with them, for the third season, even as we barely began the second.

Now, I said to myself: "Mr. Grower, it's time to get ready for another season of Women and Weed."

About the Author

H e was born in New York and raised in New York. He attended private elementary and middle school, and went to a public high school, city college, and then to the university, all located in New York. I guess you could call him a "New Yorker."

His views about life were shaped by life in New York City. He learned to eat fast, walk fast, talk fast, think fast, and live fast. To him, New York is the most cosmopolitan city in the world. It has the most diverse amalgam of languages, ethnicities, and foods. Life is unpredictable in New York.

Raised by New York stories are as much about New York as it is about the author. Enjoy the stories, smell the aroma of life as it moves through the five boroughs.

For all inquiries regarding
Raised by New York,
please contact the
author,
Herve Bebele,
at the following e-mail:
harveyhutter@gmail.com.

45859538R00130

Made in the USA
Middletown, DE
25 May 2019